PUFFIN BOOKS

Editor : Kaye Webb

THE SECRET OF THE MISSING BOAT

When Fanch salvaged a dinghy from a muddy inlet in the Estuary and re-named her the *Petit-Emile* he never expected to arouse so much curiosity. What business was it of the Harbour Master and the police-sergeant? After all, he had got permission from the Receiver of Wreck to take the boat.

And why was Monsieur Cosquer, who said he had come to lodge in Fanch's home for the rest and the sea air, so inquisitive about the boat? Who were the two men who beat him up? Did all this mystery tie up with the missing yacht *Berenice*? Or was everyone really searching for something more valuable?

This is one of Paul Berna's very best stories, set among the little islands of Brittany and their proud, independent inhabitants. His other Puffin books are *A Hundred Million Francs, The Street Musician, Flood Warning, The Knights of King Midas* and *The Mystery of the Cross-Eyed Man*.

This book received the Edgar Allan Poe Award for 1968.

The Secret
of the
Missing Boat

Paul Berna

TRANSLATED FROM THE FRENCH BY
JOHN BUCHANAN-BROWN

ILLUSTRATED BY
BARRY WILKINSON

Penguin Books

IN ASSOCIATION WITH THE BODLEY HEAD

Penguin Books Ltd, Harmondsworth, Middlesex, England
Penguin Books Australia Ltd, Ringwood, Victoria, Australia

—

La Voile Rouge first published in English translation by The Bodley Head 1966
Published in Puffin Books 1969
Reprinted 1971

—

—

Made and printed in Great Britain by
Cox & Wyman Ltd, London, Reading and Fakenham
Set in Intertype Period

Contents

Translator's Note

This story is set in Brittany, on the Morbihan, which in Breton means 'The Little Sea'. Most of the places mentioned are real places, though you will not find the Ile-Goulvan or the Ile-Hervé on any map outside this book.

VANNES

SAINT-GOUSTAN

SEVEN
MARSHES

SINCÉ

ÎLE-CONLEAU

LANDÔANE

SÉNÉ

LÉRANDRÉ

ROGUÉDAS

ÉTg DE
NOYALO

ÉTg DE KERNICOL

LANGLE

ÎLE DE BOÉDIC

NOYALO

ÎLE DE BOÈDE

MOUSTÉRIAN

ÎLE-GOULVAN

ISLE-D'ARZ

ÎLE-HERVÉ

MONTSARAC

COW ISLAND

LE
PASSAGE

LE
HÉZO

LA TEIGNE

ÎLE
D'HUR

LE BASON

H A N

SAINT-
ARZHEL

LA SENNE

SARZEAU

I

The *Petit-Emile*

LEAVING the darker blue of the bay behind them, the white sails surged through the narrows of Port-Navalo like a flock of seagulls on the flood tide. Fanch rounded the inner buoy which marked the channel, set a course for the nearest houses of Locmariaquer and then turned to watch the yachts coming back to their moorings at Larmor-Baden, Arradon and Ile-Conleau.

By comparison, the *Petit-Emile* was very much of an ugly duckling with her shabby black hull, stubby mast and dark red sail. Fanch's was a small fishing-boat, hardly bigger than a dinghy, carrying a single lugsail, but his hand on the tiller never faltered as he negotiated the tricky currents and cross-currents inshore or when sudden squalls blew in from the open sea.

Lise was sitting in the bows of the *Petit-Emile*. Slim and sun-burned, she looked towards the shore. The white houses with their blue slate roofs were closer now and she could see the tip of the pier and the harbour, lined with visitors who had come to watch the first regatta of the summer.

'Fanch,' said Lise anxiously, 'you'd better put me off behind the headland – or anywhere along the beach. It'll only mean walking to Aunt Annick's over the sands.'

'No,' Fanch retorted, 'that eel is to heavy for you to carry far. I'll tie up at the end of the harbour and then you can go up the hard.'

'Well then, watch out. You'll be lucky if you don't run into someone you don't want to meet in all that crowd.'

Fanch chuckled to see her so scared.

'I'm safe aboard the *Petit-Emile*. They can't touch me here!'

Lise shrugged.

'Don't forget old Blackbeard's always on the look-out for you. If he gets his hands on you, you can say good-bye to freedom ... and to the *Petit-Emile*. I suppose you'd think it a big joke if you finished your trip locked up in a boarding-school.'

Fanch laughed. His encounters with Monsieur Cogan, the schoolmaster of Saint-Arzhel, had turned him into an outlaw, but the disgrace spiced his water-gipsy wanderings with excitement. Whose fault was it, anyway? The ninety-six Breton saints to whom Mamm Guidic prayed should have arranged matters differently. For example, only a month before, it had so happened that, although the Ministry of Education were unaware of it, one of their exams had coincided with a most important natural phenomenon – a bore tide. It had not taken Fanch more than two seconds to make up his mind. While his schoolfellows were racking their brains over the Maths paper, he had been far up the river above Noyalo exploring a forsaken piece of marshland which was only covered once in three years by this particularly high tide.

While high water lasted, the *Petit-Emile* had cleft a path through a weird watery forest, flocks of strange seabirds breaking from under her bows with angry squawks. There were few greater excitements for Fanch than these brief glimpses of hidden territory that might be revealed at any hour of the day or night by the capricious movements of the ever-present ocean.

Fanch had never envied other people. At fourteen he was king of the Little Sea, the 'Morbihan'. Mamm Guidic and Uncle Job were not the only ones to say so, nor Lise alone in thinking it. The old fishing-captains who still used

the red-sailed, traditional Breton fishing-boats known as
'sinagots' would nobly doff their caps as they passed him,
for they respected his knowledge of the Little Sea and his
skill in handling the *Petit-Emile*.

As the boat nudged the hard, Lise jumped out and made
her way up to the quayside, the conger slung uncomfor-
tably over her right shoulder, its tail tapping her
ankles.

'Don't stay too long,' Fanch warned her. 'We've only a
couple of hours of the flood-tide left and we should be
getting back to the islands.'

There must have been some fifty strollers still idling
along the quayside, stopping every now and then to admire
the tall masts swaying on the tide. Nobody bothered to
glance at the *Petit-Emile*. The minutes slipped peacefully
away; the car-park by the sea-front gradually emptied;
the shadow of the houses lengthened across the square –
and still Lise did not return. Every so often Fanch looked
up, his keen eyes sweeping the last few stragglers for the
sinister wedge of black beard which threatened his inde-
pendence.

Monsieur Cogan was not there, but the forces of the
Law appeared in another guise that evening. Suddenly
they were there, unheralded, almost like old friends, and
nobody near would have guessed that the owner of the
little black boat was in any way worried by the sight of
them.

'Ahoy there, sailor!' a voice called from above him.
'Secure that old tub of yours, and come up here for a
minute. We want to talk to you.'

Five men were standing on the wharf just above the
hard, sharply silhouetted against the glare of the sunset.
Fanch screwed up his eyes and raised a hand to shade
them. The first person he recognized was the largest of
the five, Monsieur Tanguy, the Harbour Master. He was

known to everyone as 'Old Hogshead'. Next to him was
the redoubtable Customs Officer, Stephani, lean and dark.
A little apart were two gentlemen who looked very miserable and out-of-place in their suits and collars and ties. At
the end of the line stood a policeman, a bland expression
on his face and an inquisitive gleam in his eyes which
boded no good for Fanch.

'Are you coming?' called Old Hogshead.

'I can hear you quite well from here,' Fanch answered,
unabashed. 'What do you want?'

'These gentlemen are not going to get their feet wet,
just to have a closer look at you,' the quick-tempered Harbour Master snapped, going very red in the face. 'You
come up here, and be quick about it, or the sergeant will
have you up by the ears!'

'I shouldn't count on that,' Fanch said, firmly but politely.

He was about to slip his moorings and run with the tide,
leaving poor Lise to find her own way home, when he
thought better of it. After all, the five men on the quayside
were not the usual sort of jokers who had taken a drink too
many on a Sunday evening. He went up to them as though
performing a penance, his feet bare, his eyes to the ground.
There were plenty of holes in his striped singlet, but
neither this nor his patched pair of jeans could hide his
vigour.

'What's his name?' asked one of the strangers.

Monsieur Tanguy told them Fanch's pedigree, with no
concern whatsoever for his feelings.

'François Jouin. But everyone calls him Fanch. His surname doesn't really matter – he's a foundling. He lives with
old Madame Guidic. She has a farm on the Ile-Goulvan
across the bay. Been a foster-mother for the Welfare
people for years. She must have had at least thirty kids
through her hands, but this one took her fancy more than

all the rest put together. She's been allowed to look after him until he leaves school.'

'The result's nothing out of the ordinary,' one of the gentlemen remarked drily. 'What do you plan to do when you're sixteen?'

'I'll stay and help Madame Guidic. Can't do anything else, can I? Not that there isn't plenty to do on the island. Anyway, I like it there.'

'Only if you can get away from it ten or twelve times a day,' put in the Customs man. 'The old woman can't even keep you in her sight for more than two hours at a time.'

They turned away. Fanch was puzzled. The men were looking at the little boat below them, rocking on the tide and tugging at her moorings. There was silence for several minutes; then Monsieur Tanguy began to speak again, and at last Fanch had some inkling of what interested his five interrogators.

'I wouldn't know the *Petit-Emile* these days,' Old Hogshead announced. 'It may be my imagination, but she seems to have grown into a much finer boat in the last fortnight.'

There was a threat in his sarcasm. Fanch said nothing.

'Anyone can see from here that your sail is good canvas,' the Harbour Master went on. 'That's luxury for a little tub like yours. You couldn't have bought it with the pocket-money Mamm Guidic allows you ... Now, where did that sail come from?'

'I haven't a clue,' Fanch answered. 'It came down the northern channel from the river mouth at Vannes and the tide left it high and dry on the mud-bank by our island one morning. On Goulvan we're right in the way of anything brought down from the north and it's not often worth having, either.'

The Customs man and the police-sergeant deigned to smile, but the two strangers were icy.

'You don't dispose of jetsam as easily as that,' Monsieur Tanguy said severely. 'Before taking charge of it, you should have asked the nearest Receiver of Wreck what he had to say about it. Did you do that?'

'Of course I did. I went over to Langle the very same day to show Monsieur Riou the sail and he let me keep it. It was a middle jib and its head was in ribbons. I cut it down to fit my boom and now I've got a brand new sail that catches the wind a lot better than my old one.'

Monsieur Tanguy's eyes brooded on the little black boat which seemed to mock him as it rocked on the tide. Once more he frowned and continued his examination.

'And you've got a new mast, too, unless I'm growing shortsighted. Don't you deny it, the old one was like a broom handle.'

'Of course!' Fanch grinned. 'It's not much use having a new sail if you haven't got anything strong enough to carry it.'

'And a nice bit of timber, too!' Monsieur Stephani remarked as he looked at the mast in admiration. 'New varnish, as well. Whew! A millionaire's yacht isn't better rigged. Own up, now! That mast cost you a good bit more than the sail.'

Fanch remained silent.

'Course it didn't!' Old Hogshead guffawed. 'Bet the north channel delivered him the mast as well, cost, carriage and Customs free.'

'No, it didn't. It was the east channel, from the River Noyalo,' Fanch explained innocently. 'It's not my fault. The mast was washed up on the little bit of sand opposite Cow Island that's only uncovered at low water. Of course I towed it over to Langle and Monsieur Riou gave me his honest opinion.'

'And just what did the old boy have to say?'

'He said, "You keep your stick of wood and carry on

combing the Ile-Goulvan. It's a good spot. With a bit of patience, one of these days you'll end up salvaging a schooner!" '

The Customs man and the police-sergeant roared with laughter, but the two strangers failed to appreciate the joke and they simply gazed, horrified, at the black boat. Monsieur Tanguy, meanwhile, completed his attack, and his third remark caught Fanch off guard.

'I said a moment ago that I could hardly recognize your old tub. I wasn't joking, either. We've dealt with the mast and the sail – that leaves the hull. The size of it begins to make me blink. My word! The *Petit-Emile* seems to have gained a good three feet overall and as much again across the beam since she was last here . . . How do you explain that?'

Fanch took a deep breath and bravely began his explanation.

'It's a different hull,' he admitted, with a hang-dog grin. 'I found it about a month ago when we had that bore tide.'

'Where?' Monsieur Tanguy cut in.

'I'd gone right up on the tide round about Saint-Goustan. There's a silted-up channel above the oyster-parks. The boat was in the mud up to her gunwales and covered with reeds. It took me a couple of hours to refloat her and a couple more to tow her over to the beach at Langle.'

'And I'll bet the old wrecker was waiting for you smoking his pipe.' Monsieur Stephani raised a laugh.

Fanch frowned.

'Monsieur Riou looked at the lists from the Ministry of Marine and rang up the sailing clubs and the oyster-farmers and the Receiver of Wreck on the Isle-d'Arz. But there wasn't a boat missing, so in the end it was left on his hands. So he let me use it for the time being. The next day

I repainted it and shifted all my gear from one boat to the other and no one noticed the difference.'

'Except me!' Old Hogshead was triumphant.

The police-sergeant, who was enjoying the situation, now took up the running.

'What it boils down to,' he said, 'is this: there's not a scrap of the *Petit-Emile* left.'

'Only the tiller and the rudder,' said Fanch calmly. 'And the name of course. I repainted that on the stern.'

Suddenly Monsieur Tanguy's expression changed.

'You're not having us on, are you, Fanch? Remember, I've only got to say the word and the authorities will confiscate your boat. Then, if you want to get back to your old Mamm, you'll have to swim for it.'

Fanch lowered his head and gritted his teeth. Out of the corner of his eye he measured the distance between himself and the *Petit-Emile*. There was a muttered exchange between the Harbour Master and the two strangers and then Monsieur Tanguy turned to deliver his verdict.

'Fanch,' his voice was serious, 'chance has given you these three bits of salvage, but it hasn't given you complete possession of them. To be precise, you are entitled to only a third of their value. I'm perfectly prepared to believe that Monsieur Riou has persuaded the Town Council of Langle to make you a gift of the rest, and I won't argue with their generosity. But you mustn't forget the fact that the three parts of the *Petit-Emile* once, and fairly recently, each belonged to somebody else, and who knows if it wasn't to one and the same person. If you should ever happen to run across that person, remember the law about returning lost property or you'll be in for a nasty time. We're fairly certain you won't lose any sleep over this warning, but all the same, keep your eyes open when you're at the helm, and if you run into trouble, don't forget to turn to your old friend, Monsieur Tanguy.'

After one last glance at the *Petit-Emile,* the men made off along the quay. Thoughtfully Fanch climbed down to the boat; he did not feel really at ease until he was aboard. It was now half-tide and the current was flowing against the pierhead strongly.

Soon Lise reappeared, nursing a giant apple-pie from her Aunt Annick's oven.

'Shall we eat it here, or when we're under way?' she asked greedily. 'It's still quite warm ...'

Suddenly Fanch's nerve snapped.

'For goodness sake, sling it aboard and let's get out of here! The harbour people have been bothering me with a stack of questions about the boat and I jolly nearly had to leave you behind to get out of their clutches.'

'Help! Then I'd have had to make my own way home on the Sunday ferry to Arz. The farmers round Ménezic always keep a punt at the bottom of their potato-fields but it would have taken me half an hour or so to drift down to the Ile-Hervé.'

'And what about the *Petit-Emile?*' Fanch grumbled. 'You couldn't care less about her. Any day now, a policeman and some Government clerk will be waiting in a couple of feet of water, all ready to grab her when I come in to land, and that'll be me fixed. The next day a Welfare Officer will send me off to some stinking farm the other side of Landivisiau ... and how would I like that!'

Angrily he shoved off from the hard. At once a puff of wind swelled the red sail and gently nudged them through the eddies in the channel. Seriously worried about the fate of the *Petit-Emile,* Fanch told his story.

'All you need have done,' Lise joked, 'was to have painted her white and bought yourself a yachting-cap. Nobody would have touched you then – visitors are sacred.'

'But I'm not a boat-thief!' Fanch protested.

'No, but you let some idiots think you are, just to give yourself a little importance, and now everyone believes it's true. One of these days you'll find yourself hauled in by the police under some law or other that's three hundred years old.'

'But I put myself in the clear with the Receiver of Wreck at Langle.'

'Fanch, be your age! Langle is on the other side of the bay. It's another country. If you really want a quiet life, keep close to Goulvan.'

'The *Petit-Emile*'s seaworthy enough to go anywhere. The new one, I mean.'

'I know you do,' Lise answered mockingly. 'And I suppose it's because she draws too much that you can't take her through the narrows by Port-Blanc or Ile-Conleau?'

Fanch flushed angrily.

'Trying to get under my skin, are you?'

'No, just my way of putting things. I know she barely draws a foot of water. But maybe there is something queer about her, which Old Hogshead's been careful not to tell you.'

'*What?*' Fanch asked, as he stared at the new mast, the swelling sail and the dark bow breasting the tide. 'Jetsam belongs to the first person who finds it. I never tried to sell the things, and they were enough for me to refit a new *Petit-Emile* in under a week . . . I'm not getting all that out of it,' he added with a laugh. 'And the only things I disturbed were a couple of moorhens nesting in the bows.'

'But you've got to admit we felt far more at home in the old boat.'

Lise was only just twelve. Despite its poverty, life on the islands of the Little Sea was healthy and it had made her tough without repressing the high spirits natural in someone of her age. Although she had a forgiving nature, she was scrupulously honest in matters of right and wrong.

Fanch dropped his eyes before her uncompromising stare.

'Well, this is the last time we sail together,' he said spitefully. 'From now on you'd better find someone else if you want to leave your oyster-park.'

Ten minutes later, the *Petit-Emile* shot like an arrow through the gateway of the Morbihan, the wooded spur of the Ile-Longue and Pember Point. Before them stretched the broad blue of the bay, with its ever-changing horizon, its isles and innumerable reefs now turning gold in the setting sun, and its sails sparkling against the green-tinged sky.

Lise and Fanch made up their differences in a joint assault on the apple-pie, as the *Petit-Emile* sped bravely on, passing a couple of drifters which had missed the tide. Monsieur Tanguy's warning still echoed in Fanch's ears and made the loneliness of the voyage home even more disturbing. From now on each trip would be a real adventure, with this nameless peril lurking among the innocent-seeming islands.

'Let's get things straight,' Lise was saying. 'Whether you like it or not, the real owner's going to take back the *Petit-Emile* from you, and the only salvage he'll pay you is a good hiding. That's the worst that can happen to you ...'

'A wreck's a wreck,' Fanch answered obstinately. 'It's just too bad for the man who loses his boat. The sea does what it likes with it and gives it to someone else, sometimes still in one piece, but more often in thirty-six. I'm not giving up my share so easily. Whoever's on the look-out for it, is going to have an awful long wait before he gets his hooks on to her.'

To port they watched the woods and gardens of the Isle-aux-Moines slip past, the scent of flowers drifting on the wind. The fastest yachts had scattered to the north, towards the bay of Arradon and the pink-walled houses of Roguedas. Packed with visitors and country-folk in their Sunday best, the launch from Vannes passed far astern of the *Petit-Emile*. Soon the barren shores of the Isle-d'Arz loomed up on the horizon like a long white wall. As night came on, the wind lessened.

Fanch made no mistake as he picked his course among the almost invisible network of currents. Wooded or barren, the islets were strung out abeam, sometimes in clusters, sometimes opening to reveal a wide seascape which gave the illusion of the open sea. The last remaining sails flamed red in the setting sun and then went out one by one as they disappeared into their coves. There was a dull chugging astern as two sardine boats returned to Vannes on the tide. Slowly they gained on the *Petit-Emile*, giving her a friendly toot on the siren as they came past.

When the squat shapes of the sardine boats had vanished over the horizon, Fanch and Lise were left alone on the water. The wind came only in puffs to make the yard creak against the mast. Then it died away altogether and the dusk drained the empty sea of all its colour.

'The tide's still running, but only just!' Fanch laughed. 'If you'd spent another hour with your Aunt Annick, we'd have had to row home with a candle in the bows.'

Lise was silent, looking ahead for the two islands on which their respective homes stood. Their presence could be guessed from afar by the strong smell of wood-smoke floating on the lazy air. By now the shimmering expanse of water had turned milky white with only the slightest touch of colour on the far side of the bay. The Ile-Hervé was the first to come into sight, with its squares of stakes marking the oyster-parks, the yellow house masked by the tamarisks, the rough grass broken by clumps of briar and tall bracken and the solitary pine standing like the mast at the end of a raft. The island was little over a quarter of a mile long, but the shallows which surrounded it made it ideal for oyster-farming.

Fanch brought the *Petit-Emile* alongside the two punts belonging to Monsieur Jégo, Lise's father. She stepped overboard into a foot of water and splashed ashore. The light from the windows was softened by the screening tamarisks. At last Lise reached the sandy track leading to the house. When she looked back to the shore, the boat was outlined slack-sailed like a derelict against the paleness of the waves, and the sight of it made her shiver.

'Ahoy, Fanch!' she called. 'Don't lose any sleep over who owns your boat. Blackbeard must have started that story just to scare you.'

'That's what you think! Monsieur Tanguy wouldn't have got the police-sergeant and the Customs man out for a little thing like that. It looked as though they were waiting for me. Someone must have been keeping a watch on us as we were coming through the narrows.'

'Well then, here's my advice. Shove the new boat out on the ebb-tide and say good-bye to her. The others will forget all about it in the end.'

Fanch pulled an oar from under the thwart and stuck it into the mud to shove the boat off.

'I don't mean to lumber myself with a little coward,' he shouted angrily. 'You haven't even started to grow up, and I'm bursting out of my rags all over. Ever since the end of the winter I've been looking for something to replace that old boat of mine. Now I've found it, but I need somebody my own size as crew ... Good night!'

He let himself drift with the tide which was still running sluggishly towards the far side of the bay. It was nearly high water and all around the land looked like a thin layer of cloud against the sky. About half a mile to the north of the Ile-Hervé lay the Ile-Goulvan, a larger and greener island. From seaward the tall rocky cliffs of its western shore completely hid the farm-buildings, the woods and the fields. You had to follow the line of the cliffs and clear Sow Point before you suddenly saw the amazing island oasis lying at the head of a sandy cove.

Fanch stopped whistling. There, moored alongside the big flat-bottomed boat used to carry stuff for the farm, was a blue motor-boat. As he came nearer, he saw that it was the *Pierre-et-Paul*, belonging to Monsieur le Glohec, a childhood friend of Uncle Job, living in retirement at Saint-Arzhel. There was nothing unusual about a visit from him, but sometimes the old boy did a taxi service for the town hall, the neighbours or the school, and it could be that he had just landed Blackbeard on Goulvan.

Fanch ran the *Petit-Emile* aground near Sow Rock – even at low tide he could float off from his mooring – quietly lowered sail and furled it carefully.

A properly surfaced road ran up to the farm through a copse of oak and elm. Madame Guidic stood in the yard gateway, sharply outlined like a statue against a still mauve patch of sky. She always wore black, unrelieved by any touch of colour. Her white hair drawn up under a peasant cap accentuated the bony structure of her face, tanned yellow by the wind and sun.

'Welcome home!' she called, with a hint of sarcasm in her voice. 'It's only a false alarm. Monsieur le Glohec has brought us a lodger. He'll be staying for two or three weeks.'

'Did you have a good look at him?' Fanch asked suspiciously. 'Blackbeard would stoop to anything to get me over to Saint-Arzhel every day and into that wretched school of his. Why, he'd even make friends with the parish priest. Well, I'm not going to spend the whole summer locked up with either of them!'

'You've nothing to worry about, my lad. It's only a

gentleman from Paris who wants a rest and some sea air. He seems quite nice ... We've put him in the guest-room. You'll see him when he comes down to dinner.'

He gave her a kiss and they walked hand in hand towards the lime-washed farmhouse. There were two full generations between the foundling and the old woman of the islands who had replaced his own mother. Fanch, however, never noticed the slow decay which age had worked on the bent and broken figure of the old lady. To him Mamm Guidic was always the same. Weak though she was growing in body, her heart still beat strongly and imprinted on her face the same smile, the same loving watchful expression which he had always known.

Uncle Job and Monsieur le Glohec were sitting in the farm kitchen drinking a glass of white wine by the light of the big copper oil-lamp which hung from the rafters. The boy's uneasy expression made them laugh. His three years' game of hide-and-seek with Blackbeard-Cogan had already become local legend.

Old Monsieur le Glohec had to leave almost immediately if he was to get back to Saint-Arzhel before darkness closed in completely. Uncle Job went down to the boat with him and then returned to busy himself among the outbuildings in which the Ile-Goulvan's herd of fifteen cattle were peacefully chewing the cud.

'I'm going to make pancakes,' Mamm Guidic told Fanch, 'so you can get a move on and lay the table. As long as we've got our visitor, all four of us will use the best Quimper china . . . So mind you don't break any plates!'

The door to the farmyard had been left wide open. It was growing cooler now and the vivid green of the fig-trees was dimming in the grey of the dusk. As he leant over the table, Fanch sensed a movement behind him. Turning round, he saw a tall shape outlined in the doorway. Alarums and excursions had for some time been in the air he breathed, so he said nothing and swallowed his words of welcome.

Five or six slow strides brought their lodger into the golden circle of lamplight. He was a man of about forty. He was thin and very sun-burned, and his dark eyes glinted shrewdly under brows which formed a thick black line above his beaky nose. His singlet had been washed so often that all the colour had gone out of it and his old green linen slacks seemed to have been preserved especially for his island holiday.

Fanch thought he looked rather too fit for someone who was supposed to be needing a rest.

'Lost your tongue?' grumbled Mamm Guidic. 'Say good-evening to Monsieur Cosquer.'

Fanch mumbled a greeting and shook hands with the lodger, who had a grip like iron. Monsieur Cosquer was obviously eager to get on the right side of the simple folk whom he had chosen to look after him.

'Since we're all one happy family,' he said with a booming laugh, 'I'm not going to stand on my dignity. I'd like you all to call me Benny – it's the name my pals in the oil-fields in Libya gave me. I'm a geologist, a sort of diviner who uses sticks of dynamite to find oil-wells.'

From his surname one might have supposed that he came from Lower Brittany, but oddly, although there was the trace of an accent in his speech, it was not a Breton one. Mamm Guidic seemed impressed, but Fanch sensed that all this show of friendship did not quite ring true. He pointed up at the reddish ball of copper hanging by polished chains from the rafters, its gleaming glass shade spreading warmth and light.

'The only oil on Goulvan is in that lamp,' he said quizzically, 'but don't let that stop you prospecting on Cow Island. Mamm really would be glad to have an oil-

well next door for her lamp and so would Uncle for the engine in his punt.'

Benny roared with laughter. Uncle Job had just brought in a basket of new-laid eggs. Slow-moving and taciturn, he pushed his Naval Reservist's cap to the back of his head.

'Well, Monsieur,' he said shyly, 'if it's peace and quiet you're after, you'll find it here. And if ever you should want to go over to the mainland, you've got the choice of my punt or the *Petit-Emile*.'

'The *Petit-Emile*?' Benny's bushy eyebrows lifted.

'Fanch's boat. He's put it together with the bits and pieces of driftwood he's salvaged from the channel. Or very nearly, that is. It's not much of a boat when you see it at its moorings, but once Fanch takes the helm, why, the wind seems to change a point or two and the tides run specially for him. Even Monsieur Riou, the oldest fisherman at Port Langle, can't explain it! He's amazed by it all.'

Benny was sceptical and tried to be smart.

'Who is the *Petit-Emile* named after?'

'Not me,' Fanch answered harshly. 'I didn't even know him.'

Mamm Guidic had slowly and almost reluctantly moved away towards the huge, old fashioned chimney-piece whose monumental canopy filled the far wall. Uncle Job bent down to count his new-laid eggs once more, hiding his embarrassment. The stranger realized too late that he had stumbled on one of the family's sorrows.

He remained silent for a moment and lit a cigarette.

The old woman had once had a son Emile who had died as a small child. Her husband had died soon afterwards, and she had made a home with her brother. From then on she had squandered her mother-love on foundlings from the State Orphanage, until at last she had con-

29

centrated it all upon a fair-haired, passionate boy, come from goodness knows where and baptized in a hurry. And he at last was making a full return for all this love. Once Fanch was old enough to venture out on the water alone, he had carried the name of the brother he had never known to the four corners of the bay. He showed his allegiance to his adopted mother by a devotion which was unsought on her side but which ensured that her name would survive in this forgotten corner of the country.

If the traditions of the farmers and fishermen clinging to their little islands were to endure, plenty of women as proud and courageous as Madame Guidic were needed to pass on to some at least of their children a taste for a way of life at once free yet circumscribed by its natural surroundings, and to teach them that the true wages of the most unrewarding toil are the joys of living, joys soon dulled in the environment of a great city. Fanch was of this breed. She knew it; and the boy's natural hatred of restraint made her the more indulgent towards him.

The oil man puffed at his cigarette and turned to Fanch with well-mannered interest.

'I've done a bit of sailing in my time. I wouldn't mind crewing for you if you'd let me.'

'Depends on your weight.' Fanch was abrupt. 'I'm telling you, the day Blackbeard steps over her gunwales, you can bet the *Petit-Emile* will go down like a stone.'

Mamm Guidic glided towards them carrying a steaming tureen. Cautioned by the sudden chill in the conversation he had caused a few minutes before, Benny no longer dared to ask rash questions. However, seeing smiling faces around him, he said breathlessly:

'And who is this Blackbeard?'

Uncle Job told him the whole story and at once the atmosphere grew noticeably easier.

'First thing tomorrow,' their lodger promised, rapping

on the table, 'we'll set sail for Saint-Arzhel and I'll sort out this schoolmaster of yours for you!'

'I should wait till you're really fit again,' said Fanch.

There was a burst of laughter; Mamm Guidic served the soup; and thus, on a clear June evening, adventure came to the island.

2

The Seven Marshes

LIKE all the other rooms in the farmhouse, the walls of the spare bedroom were whitewashed, but the dark, polished wood of the antique furniture gave it a touch of distinction. There was a separate door leading out into the yard where the fig-trees grew and the two huge windows looked south-east over the ever-changing seascape of the bay.

The far-off lowing of cattle, with sounds of movement growing fainter in the distance, woke Benny at four o'clock the next morning. He got out of bed, drew back the curtains and stayed looking out of the window for quite a while.

The tide rules the daily life of the semi-circle of coast between Arradon and Saint-Arzhel, alternately raising and lowering the shimmering surface of the bay. At high tide, the horizon encircles a calm sea studded with tiny grey or green islets, the antechamber of the wide ocean. But at low water, the ebb slowly reveals a drowned landscape which seems suddenly to rise stark against the sky. A thousand secret paths seem to link the mainland once more with the ruins sunk for ten or twelve centuries in the mud of the tidal channels.

The midsummer sun had scarcely risen and the first light tinged with pink the black mud-banks exposed by the ebb. Benny leaned out of the window, unable to take his eyes off an extraordinary sight. There were Mamm Guidic's fifteen Friesians swaying in single file across the half-mile or so of the arm of sea which separated them from their pasture on Cow Island. A shaggy dog chased up and down the line stirring the laggards, plunging every so often into deep pools amid a flurry of barks. The fair-haired boy brought up the rear, swinging a stout stick. His whistles to the dog and his shrill calls to the cattle carried through the clear air. Except for the occasional cock-crow, the Ile-Goulvan still slumbered on.

Benny dressed hurriedly, crossed the yard and made for the gate. Standing at the end of the road, at first he thought that the tide had laid bare the entire sea-bed around the headland, but as he approached the shore he soon saw that there was plenty of water by Sow Point. Here the outflow from Vannes and Noyalo converged to build up against the pier of the headland and to sweep below the sheer cliffs of the western side of the island. Thus the neighbours used to say, not without a trace of envy, that Goulvan always had one foot in the water.

Fanch's dinghy and the big black punt strained against their moorings on the ebb. The old oil-drum they used as a mooring buoy lay close to its dead block on the sand. The stern of the heavy punt was firmly aground, but the *Petit-Emile* still floated free, bobbing on the wave-lets.

Benny walked slowly down the beach to the edge of the water. He tugged on the line and the *Petit-Emile* grounded gently in front of him. He touched nothing, but looked her over two or three times, closely examining the hull, mast and the carefully furled sail lying across the thwarts. He whistled softly, but his unsmiling face gave no hint of his thoughts. Occasionally a larger wave drove the boat towards him, for the tide had started to turn. A moment or so later he suddenly stopped whistling, knelt down and peered closely at the roughly painted hull.

At that very moment Fanch came down the road and caught him bending under the bows of the *Petit-Emile*.

Fanch laughed loudly at the antics of the visitor, who started to his feet.

'Back already? ... What have you done with your cows?'

'I've left the dog to look after them,' Fanch explained. 'He's used to it and can manage by himself. Uncle Job goes over every high tide to milk them and then takes the churns straight over to Saint-Arzhel. We leave the cattle over there for ten days to a fortnight at a time to let the grazing on our own fields recover a bit ... But you shouldn't have got up so early,' he added solicitously.

'Who asked you to keep an eye on me?' Benny said coldly.

'Nobody. Only when I came home I saw your door was open and if Mamm doesn't shut it for you all the cats in the place will be clawing your eiderdown or purring on your pillow ... What were you looking at?' he added, pointing to the boat.

'Whoever scraped and repainted your hull didn't do a very good job of it,' Benny answered cuttingly. 'You can see patches of white paint under the coat of black ... Was the boat stolen?'

'Not by me,' Fanch replied, unperturbed, 'and anyway I don't see what it's got to do with you. Actually, they wouldn't give you two hundred francs for her over at Vannes or Ile-Conleau and round here none of the locals have been falling over themselves for her, nor have the visitors ...'

Their mutual dislike was growing. Benny was the first to try to put things on a more friendly footing.

'Don't be offended by my curiosity. I'm fascinated by everything here, it's all so new and strange. I hope we'll be able to sail over to Noyalo sometime soon.'

Fanch noticed that these efforts at politeness only made Benny's beaky features a little uglier.

34

'Don't be in too much of a hurry,' he said, his thoughts far away. 'I've got plenty to do here and elsewhere, and it's riskier for me every trip I make. I can't set foot on the mainland before Monsieur Cogan comes bowling up in his car. He sticks so close you'd think he'd got a naval range-finder fixed on me from the school-window four miles away.'

'Bad as that then?'

'Worse! I hope I never fall into his crazy hands. He'd pull all sorts of strings; Mamm Guidic wouldn't be able to do a thing for me. They'd shove me straight into an orphanage and that would be the end of me.'

Benny guffawed.

'Come off it! I'm sure you're making a mountain out of a molehill! If all truants had it as easy as you have, the roads wouldn't be safe in the rush to get away!'

Fanch did not move a muscle.

'Bluff!' Benny went on. 'Cogan hasn't an ounce of real authority outside the school. He shouldn't take people in by pretending he has. It only needs someone to put him properly in his place, and then he'll leave you in peace.'

Fanch looked disbelieving. He turned towards the sea. The mooring-buoy and the punt were both afloat now. The tide was pushing the *Petit-Emile* towards her master.

'Taking me with you?' Benny asked when he saw the boy jump aboard.

'Not this morning,' Fanch said. 'I'm going across to the Ile-Hervé; our neighbours, the Jégos, are waiting for me at the oyster-parks.'

He hauled in his mooring-line, and looked hard at Benny, standing motionless on the sands of the cove. They studied each other for a moment with a curiosity which was almost insulting.

'I've seen you somewhere before,' the boy said suddenly. 'In the last two or three days.'

'Perhaps you have,' Benny answered calmly. 'Where?'

'I think it was the day before yesterday, on the end of the pier at Le Logéo. You were sitting on a suitcase watching the yachts put to sea. There were a couple of big blokes with you.'

'Congratulations,' said Benny. 'You certainly keep a sharp pair of eyes in your head. Yes, some friends had given me a lift in their car and just dropped me off. I was looking round for somewhere to stay.'

'Didn't take you long to find your way to Goulvan,' Fanch remarked. 'Mamm sometimes takes people in, but the only ones who know that are the locals at Saint-Arzhel.'

'I've the knack of finding good places, that's all.'

On this note they parted. The *Petit-Emile*'s red sail

soon vanished behind Sow Rock and the visitor walked back to the farm, now stirring to life in the full morning sunshine.

Benny's behaviour both embarrassed and puzzled his hosts. He had come ashore from the *Pierre-et-Paul* carrying a shabby little suitcase tied up with a piece of string, a black raincoat slung across his shoulder, and wearing a singlet, green linen slacks and a pair of canvas shoes. He was never seen wearing anything better, and anyway his case was too small to hold more than a change of underwear and his night things. On his first morning Benny paid for a fortnight's board and lodging in cash to old Madame Guidic, whom he called Mamm from the very beginning.

'This will do for the time being,' he said. 'Of course an extra week would do me the world of good. I need to put on a stone in weight and I shan't lose this nervous tic overnight. It's not just a comfortable bed and plenty of good food I need, but peace and quiet as well.'

So he was left to himself. The old lady moved round the farmhouse like a shadow; Uncle Job was always either in the vegetable garden or the fields, while the only time Fanch put in an appearance was for meals. Afterwards he would vanish again, without a word, without a smile, always on the trot. Their lodger ate like a horse, said very little and spent most of his time sleeping, either in his room or in the shade of the fig-trees in the yard. Mamm Guidic often found him in the kitchen staring at a map, yellow with age, which was hanging framed upon the wall.

'Don't you trust that,' the old woman told him. 'It's very old and full of mistakes.'

'That's just what interests me,' Benny answered, still studying it. 'The present-day coastline's so artificial, now the locals have filled in all the coves with their wretched oyster-parks.'

He had the air of being there just to wait for something, quite patiently, the expectation being enough to fill his days of idleness. At high tide when the sea stretched as far as the eye could see, he would walk slowly and unweariedly round the island, from the spinney to the heath, then along the cliff-tops to the pine trees on the south beach, returning by way of the meadows and the kitchen-garden with its wind-break of thick tamarisks. Uncle Job, busy with the hay or the strawberries or the potatoes, would hear him whistling, the sound floating across the island, now loud, now dying away in the distance, and it was as irritating as the buzz of a wasp.

Benny was waiting for the high tide of the twenty-eighth and Fanch's good pleasure. The tables could not lie, the tide would keep its appointment. As for the rest, Benny dared not rush matters.

For the last three days, their neighbours on the Ile-Hervé had been frantically busy at every low tide. In two foot of water, the chequer-board pattern of the oyster-parks become clear, the dyke-walls formed by bundles of faggots and the tiles hanging from a central picket-post in the shape of a beehive or lying horizontally on wooden frames. There had been a tremendous hurry to replace these lime-washed tiles which are used to collect the spat (the floating larvae of the oyster), to make good any rotten woodwork and to clean the great square wood-and-wire sieves, the 'ambulances' to which the baby oysters are transferred. All around were the same scenes of activity. From the Séné Peninsula to Saint-Arzhel, the local inhabitants had poured out to work on the banks exposed at low tide under the blazing sun.

The Jégos and their six workmen were barely enough for the task in hand. It had to be done at top speed to take advantage of every second of low water. Fanch and Lise worked side by side. The girl was not surprised to hear that Mamm Guidic had taken in a lodger, for all the year round, even in the winter, the islanders took in townsfolk anxious to get away from it all.

'And he's another one who comes sniffing round my boat,' Fanch said bitterly. 'I'll finish up by thinking you were right and that the *Petit-Emile* would be better off at the bottom of the sea. And he's not much of a one anyway. Mamm'll be lucky if she makes a penny out of him. He does nothing all day, eats enough for six and you can see him getting fatter all the time.'

'Has he tried anything on yet?'

'No, but I think he will.'

Lise carefully lowered into the water the ambulance which she had been cleaning and replaced its metal lid. Then her grey eyes sparkled at Fanch.

'You know the easiest way to get to the bottom of all this? Ask him if he'd like a sail round the islands. He's bound to take the opportunity either to pump you or to tell you what's on his mind. And it isn't as if you were trying to trap him or anything.'

'Of course it isn't!' Fanch laughed. 'If you ask me the boot's on the other foot, and all he's waiting for is the chance to chuck me overboard and sail off in my old boat: I've a hard enough job as it is keeping out of his way when I go home to the farm.'

'If he says yes, let's both go.'

'No, it's strictly between him and me. If you're around, he'll probably shut up like a clam.'

Fanch had sounded unimpressed, but he felt both attracted and encouraged by Lise's suggestion. She watched him for a moment without speaking, and then added abruptly:

'Just between the two of us, then, where did you find the *Petit-Emile*, the new one I mean?'

'There's no secret about it.' Fanch shrugged. 'I told Monsieur Riou, I told Uncle Job and the other evening I told Monsieur Tanguy. I found her up river, above Noyalo, in the middle of the Seven Marshes. But it's such a tangle of reed-beds that it would be hard to find the exact place again. In any case you can only sail up the river when there's an extra high tide. I haven't been back since I found the boat.'

'There's a pretty good tide tomorrow morning,' Lise said. 'Mind you don't miss it.'

Three times the cock crowed behind the empty cowshed. Benny stirred under the bedclothes, opened his eyes and got a sudden shock to see winter drifting past the ill-fitting curtains. And yet it was as warm as the evening of his arrival. He could not believe his eyes and stumbled to the window. The mainland and the islands to the east had vanished. Visibility was down to twenty yards as the gentle land-breeze covered the entire gulf with streamers of fog banked up overnight by some distant storm. At intervals the fog grew even thicker and then the entire island seemed plunged in darkness once more.

Benny had finished dressing when into his room drifted the mouth-watering smell of hot coffee. He went into the big kitchen to investigate and discovered the boy alone at the table. The lamp was unlit and the misty morning light barely outlined the fair head bent over a bowl of coffee.

'Want some?' Fanch asked and passed the pot. 'It isn't all that cold outside, but you won't get far in all that murk on an empty stomach.'

'Will it last long?'

'Not more than an hour or two. Don't panic. The first little puff of wind will blow it all away.'

Benny was touched by his rough kindliness, but the gloomy light which fell on the long table affected them

40

both. They drank their coffee without looking at one another and ate their chunks of brown bread without speaking. Outside, the sun began to break through the mist with a gleam of gold that slanted into the room and momentarily lit the old map hanging on the far wall.

'You going to work on the oyster-parks?' asked Benny, a moment later.

'At the moment,' Fanch teased him, 'Old Jégo's oysters are fast asleep twenty feet below the tide. You'd need a frogman's suit to get down there with the new tiles.'

'Then why are you up so early?'

Fanch blew into the bottom of his bowl of coffee.

'I'm going out for a sail up the gulf on the high tide,' he answered. 'Uncle Job and the Jégos pay me well enough for the work I do for them, but if I can get away in my boat, that's better than any money and I'm not very happy when anyone stops me doing it.'

He went out first and passed through the farm gate without looking back. Benny said nothing as he followed. He caught up with the boy half-way down the road to the beach under the elms dripping with moisture. They walked on together. The *Petit-Emile* turned like a top at her moorings. A gentle heave on the line brought her to Fanch.

'Want to come?' he called over his shoulder.

Purposely he had never changed the surly expression on his face. Benny winked and his face lit up.

'I don't want to force myself on you, and you can tell me to buzz off, if you like. But if I do come, you can be pretty sure you'll gain by it.'

Fanch tried to hide his astonishment.

'How?'

'To be honest, I'm not quite sure at the moment. But I've been told that you know the gulf like the back of your

41

hand, and if you act as my guide you'll be doing me a real good turn.'

'Where do you want to go?'

Benny gestured vaguely.

'You choose where. I guess we may be interested in the same spots.'

He expected some questions, but Fanch remained silent and gazed to seaward. Twenty yards away, the pale grey of the sea merged with the drifting grey of the fog-bank to blot out everything in the distance. Occasionally a window of blue and gold would open above the Ile-Goulvan, to close almost as quickly.

'We won't be able to get very far without a wind,' he said. 'The estuaries at Vannes and Vincin are too far away. And any way I've got to be back by one o'clock without fail for the low water. The Jégos are counting on me. The best thing for us to do is to let the current carry us west to Langle. If the wind gets up in the meantime we can try to push on as far as Ile-Conleau.'

'It's up to you,' Benny said serenely.

Fanch held the boat while Benny got aboard; then he cast off and jumped in. They could barely see Sow Rock, still less the wooded point which sheltered the cove from the east winds. Fanch got the oar out and sculled hard to take the boat into deep water. By now the fog had closed in all round them and the *Petit-Emile* seemed to be floating in a cloud. Benny had asked no questions, merely curling his lanky body up in the bow so as to leave the young sailor unencumbered. At last his monotonous whistling got on Fanch's nerves as he strove to catch the full force of the current.

'You won't get a wind that way,' he said impatiently. 'You'd be far better off keeping a look-out. There's a reef somewhere ahead and some of the rocks'll still be above water.'

Benny stopped at once, annoyed. They did not exchange a word as they watched for a break in the fog. The hump of the Ile-de-Lerne loomed up to port like a stranded whale and soon vanished in the murk. Every so often the boom of a siren cut through the mist and died away with a mournful wail.

Fanch was by now using the oar less to propel the boat than to keep it heading with the current. Suddenly the moisture on his left check seemed colder. The wind was starting to get up, the fog was beginning to shred in patches of light and in places the sea shone a most delicate blue. Benny heaved himself up on the thwart, his beaky nose pointing astern.

'Hoist the sail, and be quick about it!' Fanch shouted. 'This is no time to sit around.'

Hurriedly he shipped the oar, leaned over the stern to fix the rudder and slipped the tiller into place. As he did so he kept a critical eye on his hand, but Benny had not been lying and managed very creditably. A moment later the red sail was set and the *Petit-Emile* began to gather way, leaving a broad wake behind her. Rolling banks of fog sped past on either side and thinned out over the dancing waves. Then a stronger puff of wind carried the boat out of the murk into a bright blue sea and a background of land sparkling in the sunlight.

Benny was kneeling in the bow, his head level with the gunwale, scanning the green line of the horizon. He was obviously looking for his landmarks and disappointed at failing to find them.

'Where are we?'

'The current took us a bit off course in all that murk,' Fanch admitted. 'The Séné Peninsula is much further away to port, behind those two islands, Boëdic and Boëdé, and they hide the harbour of Langle. This island to starboard is Tascon.'

43

'And what's that ahead?'

Fanch knew exactly where he was, but he screwed up his eyes and pretended to scan the distant coastline.

'Those are the Narrows. They're only three hundred yards across, but the River Noyalo comes through there. She stretches for miles and miles beyond it right inland. Sometimes the tide penetrates that far . . . If you'd like,' he added politely, 'we could alter course and make for Langle. The wind's pretty steady now.'

'Better use the tide while we've got it,' Benny said drily. 'Hold your course and let's go up-river.'

A few minutes later the *Petit-Emile* shot like an arrow between the gardens of Montsarac and the white houses of Le Hézo. The estuary stretched as far as the eye could see, a waste of shimmering water unbroken except for the flight of the curlews and the drifting shadow of a cloud.

The thick hedge of reeds was broken here and there to disclose a farm set at the water's edge, a deserted mill, or a secret channel feeding sea-water to one of the many oyster-parks strung along the silent river bank. Benny was growing more and more irritable. He kept on nagging at the boy for keeping too far out in the stream. At last Fanch could bear it no longer.

'Right,' he growled, 'that's it. You can take the helm and get on with it.'

They bumped into one another getting under the sail as they changed places. Once Benny was comfortably settled in the stern he regained his cheerfulness and turned to Fanch with a friendly grin.

'I'd have thought you would have been a lot more jealous of who handled your boat. That first morning you looked black as thunder when you found me hanging around the *Petit-Emile*.'

'Well, this isn't the first time you've been aboard her, is it?' Fanch answered boldly. 'I guessed that as soon as we pushed off, just by the way you settled yourself into the bows ... Now, don't let's play games any longer ... tell me just what you're looking for.'

'Where did you salvage this boat?'

Fanch paused a moment before answering, and his reply took his opponent by surprise.

'You probably know that just as well as I do.'

His keen mind surprised Benny. The boy, after all, appeared to be only a little beachcomber and his examination of the boat could have told him nothing, yet his quick reactions and his adventurous spirit suggested he might make a fitting accomplice.

'I think we're going to be good pals,' said Benny engagingly. 'You're quite right, I knew the dinghy before you got your hands on it. But I'd be a fool to go for you because you dug it out of the mud – you must have had a fearful job doing it.'

'You'd have to get up pretty early in the morning if you wanted to catch me,' Fanch said very softly. 'This boat may only be a fifteen-footer, but I'd like to see you try and get your hands on me.'

'I shan't try,' Benny assured him. 'It's much more to my advantage to see that we get on together.'

His sinister chuckle belied his friendly words. 'Keep talking, you old crook!' Fanch thought, very much on the defensive. Suddenly he remembered Monsieur Tanguy's warnings, and the strange reception committee standing in wait for him that evening on the wharf at Locmariaquer. He almost mentioned it, but his native caution kept him silent. The crook might benefit from an ill-timed remark.

Coming well up into the wind, the *Petit-Emile* cut the dark water with the hiss of her hull against the reeds at the edge of the river. Whenever the left bank widened into a marsh, or disclosed a mysterious channel vanishing under the trees, Benny would lock the tiller against his thigh while he furtively produced a piece of paper from his pocket. From where he was sitting Fanch managed to make out that it was a chart, clumsily traced in ink, with a rash of small red spots on it, which must obviously be landmarks. Now he began to relish the situation. Minutes passed in dead silence. The current still ran strongly and the tower of Noyalo church had just vanished round a bend in the river. Benny stared round wildly.

'Where's the old brickworks at Kerguenan?' he burst out.

'We passed it five minutes ago.'

'I didn't see it!' Benny exclaimed.

'Neither did I! You can't see it at all in summer, it's hidden behind the trees ... You've been sailing in these parts before?'

Fanch was watching him out of the corner of his eye. Benny was thinking of other things.

'The boat we're in didn't get here all by herself,' he muttered. At once Fanch realized that Benny had said more than he had intended, for he made a great show of scanning the shore. At last, a little further upstream emerged a tongue of dry land. The pines which crowned it were mirrored in the water. Behind this screen, the meadows sloped gently up towards a village of which only the roof tops were visible. They had only a brief glimpse of this and then the reeds closed in to hide the shore-line. Benny grew anxious.

'From now on, you'll have to guide. Are we still on the right course?'

'It's all right as far as I'm concerned. Anyway, I could almost find my way back to the place blindfold.'

'Still some way to go?'

'No, we're almost there. When I tell you, slacken the sheet and swing her hard to starboard. Don't worry,

46

she doesn't draw enough to run aground here, and the tide's still rising.'

Fanch looked for his marks on the opposite bank, beyond the oyster-parks at Landolan. Beyond this gap rose the distant church-spire of Séné. As it came into line with the black and white buoy in the channel, the boy abruptly lowered his hand. Benny, his face tense with excitement, obeyed. The tiller swung hard over, the bows crashed through the barrier of reeds, the *Petit-Emile* gradually lost way and gently floated on the stagnant waters from which Fanch had raised her a month before.

In the morning light the lonely marshes shimmered as far as the eye could see, the dry ground lost behind a matted tangle of vegetation. Benny bit his lips and stared wildly around him.

'I don't recognize it at all,' he said, disappointed.

'Well, this is the place all right,' Fanch assured him. 'Of course this isn't the exact spot. I'll take the tiller again. You come up into the bows and keep the oar handy. If she runs aground, just push her off.'

Slowly the *Petit-Emile* nudged her way between the matted rushes and the mud-banks that made the surface of the marsh a maze. They broke through a second barrier of reeds, crossed a stretch of open water and there was the softer and fresher green of dry land ahead. The sandy point was crowned by a feathery crest of tamarisks which doubtless masked the nearby fields, proper roads and perhaps even a still-sleeping village.

'Here we are!'

'Don't you play your tricks on me,' Benny growled. 'I've never set foot in this place in my life before.'

'The boat was there. About five or six yards out in no more than a foot of water. I hauled her out of the mud with a makeshift pulley. I lashed my standing block to that tamarisk over there – the big one with its roots in the

47

water. If you think I'm telling a lie, just look over there, you can see the mark.'

Benny leaned disbelievingly out of the bows.

'All right,' he admitted, 'so you did haul her out of the water here. But you cut her out somewhere else, much higher up, and let her drift down on the tide till she ran aground here.'

'The boat was lying on the bottom!' Fanch's face was red with anger. 'And she was lying here! No one can say I cut her moorings. I'm not a pirate. She was a derelict, pure and simple. There wasn't a scrap of line on her bows or her stern.'

Benny breathed hard through his nose in an effort to keep his temper.

'You little fool, can't you see what I'm driving at?'

Fanch exploded.

'You were looking for your boat, weren't you? Well, here it is. You wanted to know where I'd found it? Well, here we are . . . What more do you want?'

Benny's eyes narrowed.

'Listen to me, my lad, when you raised this boat, the hull was painted white, and you can't deny it. I don't suppose it ever crossed your mind, did it, that it might be the dinghy from a yacht?'

Derisively Fanch shielded his eyes with his hand and peered around.

'I can't see her rigging anywhere,' he said calmly. 'But you're blocking half the horizon and I'm beginning to wonder if the real thief isn't hidden between your shoulders.'

Benny lunged at him. Fanch was easily able to dodge his fist, but the hasty movement tipped him overboard in a cloud of spray. He splashed ashore and disappeared among the tamarisks. Benny jumped after him on to the sand.

48

'Come back, Fanch!' he yelled. 'Come back at once or I'll shoot!'

'What with?'

Fanch laughed in the undergrowth. They raced through the bushes without seeing one another, and then suddenly found themselves face to face on the other side of the point. The boy brandished a sizeable cudgel and

seemed ready to use it. The exhausted Benny sat down on the ground for a moment to regain his breath.

'Listen, Fanch,' he begged, 'let's not fight. I'm only a poor wretched treasure-hunter.'

'After someone else's treasure?' Fanch teased. 'All right, I'll make peace, but you've got to tell me first what you're after.'

Benny wiped his forehead and looked up. He realized that, although Fanch couldn't be bribed to help him, the very idea of a mysterious treasure might catch the boy's imagination.

'I'm looking for something very precious and also irreplaceable.' He sighed. 'No, I'm not joking; it's the only one of its kind in the world.'

'You're having me on.' Fanch was enthralled. 'What *is* it?'

Benny rolled on to his side. A broad sweep of his hand embraced the whole expanse of marshland.

'I can't tell you that. But I know that it's somewhere in this mud-bath.'

'On your phantom yacht?'

'Perhaps . . . Help me find her!'

'I'd like to, but you'll have to tell me a bit more.'

'What do you take me for? Think I'd let you get a start on me? . . . What's this place called?'

'The Seven Channel. It leads to what used to be salt-pans until the mud got in. But a big boat displaces far too much to get up here. A cabin-cruiser might manage it on a very high tide, but that happens once in a blue moon. In any case if a boat like that had gone aground anywhere near here, the locals would soon have heard about it.'

'What are you getting at?'

'You've gone wrong twice. First of all you think too much of that map of yours. It must be a mass of mistakes. The place you're looking for can't be nearly so far up-river. And then you think that the *Petit-Emile* is really a dinghy that you've sailed before.'

'I didn't actually say that,' said Benny looking as though he didn't know what line to take.

'Then I don't believe this dinghy ever did belong to you,' Fanch insisted, 'and I have a perfect right to it.'

Lost in thought, Benny nodded. Once more he got out his map and propped his chin in his hands as he studied it.

'How long would it take us to get across to the Sincé Marshes?'

Fanch glanced through the tamarisks at the slumbering water.

'Too late now. We'll have to leave it for another time. It's almost high water and in a few minutes the ebb-tide'll start to run really fast.'

They ducked under the branches on their way back to the boat. The sun was high in the sky and beat fiercely down on this airless jungle. Benny gave a low groan when they reached the channel. The *Petit-Emile* had slipped her moorings and bobbed lazily twenty yards from the bank. But Fanch did not hesitate. He dived into the water and after a few strokes was hauling himself aboard.

'If you want to be alone,' Fanch called, 'I'll leave you here and come back to pick you up on the high tide this evening. You'd have all day to search the marshes in peace.'

Benny raised an imaginary rifle to his shoulder, took careful aim at the boy and pressed the trigger. He looked so much in earnest that for a moment Fanch could not decide whether to leave him. Then the boy sculled slowly to the shore.

'I'll do my best to help you get back "your" treasure,' he said, with a slight touch of sarcasm. 'But in return, you've got to stop threatening me and bossing me about. I'm not a kid. And I've not kept out of Blackbeard-Cogan's clutches for the last six months just to fall into the hands of a bully.'

Benny jumped aboard with obvious relief.

'Listen, Fanch,' he said seriously, 'it's not as simple as you think. I'm not the only one after this yacht and time's

51

running short. We've got to look elsewhere along this same bank, a little further upstream or downstream.'

'It just can't be done! The water will have dropped a good three feet in less than an hour from now ... Why don't you try to explore the marshes from the landward side?'

'I started by doing just that,' Benny admitted wearily, 'and it was nearly the last thing I did. You can't take a couple of steps in those reed-beds without sinking up to your neck in the mud ... What else do you suggest?'

He looked so forlorn and helpless that Fanch, excited by the prospect of hunting for lost treasure, suddenly made up his mind.

'The *Petit-Emile* can go anywhere,' he said, 'and you've got the best seaman in the gulf to guide her. Trust me. I promise you we'll come back at high tide this evening.'

3

The Voyage of the *Waikiki*

LISE was choosing those of her hundred-and-one household tasks which most frequently took her out of doors, either into the yard facing south in which Monsieur Jégo and his men were hard at work, or to the rough ground overlooking the landing stage. From here there was a splendid view of the broad sweep of the gulf with its myriad islands floating like lilies on the blue water and its changing pattern of white sails emerging from their creeks on the flood tide.

In an hour of weather as glorious as this, the black months of the Breton winter were forgotten, months when the north-westerly gales sent huge waves breaking over the low shoreline and sweeping down in the pitch dark on houses and buildings, smashing against doors and windows. When Fanch had called Lise a coward, he had been saying what in his heart of hearts he knew to be false.

Every now and then she would slip through the tamarisk hedge to glance across to the nearby Ile-Goulvan, green and fresh in the morning sun. At eight o'clock there was still no sign of the *Petit-Emile*'s sail. Eventually Madame Jégo, who was hanging her washing out to dry, began to wonder at all these comings and goings.

'Expecting Fanch? He won't be over this morning.'

'Who told you?'

'Job Guidic. He's just come across from Cow Island. Reckons the lad went off at crack of dawn with their lodger. Still, he'll be back before low water to give us a hand with those last tiles.'

53

Lise was pleased to know that Fanch had taken her advice. She needed Fanch's clumsy devotion as much as the love of her parents. They had played and grown up together, and their companionship made the happiness of their lonely life. Lise did not want to lose him and she dreaded his going as the worst thing that could happen to her. It would make the days seem twice as long, the island even more restricting and the waters around it unspeakably dreary. If she was to keep him she would have to make him more sensible; she would have to disarm the enemies who threatened his freedom. But, above all, she would have to stop him getting into such serious trouble as would lead to his being sent away for good and all. 'And this swopping of the real *Petit-Emile* for a derelict from the mud,' Lise thought sadly, 'is just the thing to do it. Until it's all cleared up, Fanch is heading for trouble even though he won't admit it.'

A gentle breeze tickled her fair hair and ruffled the sea into a paler blue. The tide was beginning to ebb. Lise saw the waters stir against the piers of the landing-stage. For the last few minutes she had heard a dull hum in the distance. She ran across the rough grass to where the solitary pine stood at the head of the Ile-Hervé.

A visitor is always a godsend to the islanders and not even the most amateur of week-end yachtsmen can disappoint their curiosity. Lise scanned the shores of the Isle-d'Arz and at last picked out the blue and white launch steering a careful course between the shoals. It swung round in a wide arc to gain the deep water channel and then headed straight for the Ile-Hervé.

The two burly men aboard the *Waikiki* had hired her from a boatman in Port-Blanc who kept a host of light craft in his sheds. She was a shallow-draught American boat, with a flat turbot-like fibre-glass hull and a powerful outboard motor. A perspex wind-shield surmounted a cabin roomy enough to take all their gear, food, clothes and the fishing tackle which served as a pretext for their trip. For the last three days they had indefatigably explored the coves of the northern coast, running the wretched *Waikiki* aground scores of times, camping on deserted islands and slowly grilling under the cloudless sky. Fredo, the more nautical of the two, kept the steering of the boat to himself. His friend Pat acted as look-out, ceaselessly sweeping the horizon with a pair of powerful binoculars whose straps seemed permanently fixed to the back of his broad neck.

'The island's inhabited,' Pat announced, the glasses still to his eyes. 'I can see a yellow house ... There are people working on the beach ... But it isn't on the map.'

'Take another look and see if you can pick out any landmarks. It's probably Cow Island.'

'That's what you think! There's not enough grass to feed a sheep.'

'Let's have a look, anyway,' Fredo decided.

The *Waikiki* surged ahead and the unknown island stood out more and more clearly from the surrounding water. Pat lowered the binoculars. A small girl stood motionless under the tall pine tree on the point and smiled as she watched them come in. She was wearing a green short-sleeved shirt and a pair of dark brown shorts which, although they had been clumsily cut down to fit her, were still far too large.

'Hullo, little girl!' Pat called in a friendly voice. 'Where on earth are we?'

'Off the Ile-Hervé,' Lise answered. 'You can land if you like, but don't stay too long, the tide drops very fast over these shoals.'

Fredo grounded the *Waikiki* gently in the shade of the pine tree and cut off the engine. Pat jumped on to the sand and fixed the anchor between two rocks. Lise felt sorry for them. Their arms and legs were as red as parboiled lobsters fresh from the pot.

'Do you need anything? The house is quite close.'

'No thanks, we've all we want,' Pat replied. 'Just paying a polite call ... And also we were wondering what you could grow on this spit of sand.'

'Hardly anything at all on the island itself,' Lise admitted with a laugh, 'but all round it my parents raise Belon oysters. Didn't you notice the posts that mark out the parks? If you'd like to, I'm sure Maman would open a couple of dozen for you, and a bottle of Muscadet to go with them.'

Her courtesy was lost on the visitors. Pat shook his head, watching the girl.

'We must do that another day,' he said ... 'But tell me, does your mother take holiday visitors by any chance? We've been wandering round the gulf looking for a very old friend of ours who said he was coming down this way for a holiday.'

Taken by surprise, Lise showed a trace of astonishment.

'Our island and house are too small for us as it is,' she said in her embarrassment. 'You'll have to look somewhere else.'

'Where?' Fredo asked off-handedly.

The girl hesitated. The two men from the *Waikiki* looked all right and their affairs were none of her business, so what was the point of hedging?

'Our neighbours on the Ile-Goulvan have had someone staying with them for the last few days. He came over on a launch from Saint-Arzhel. I don't know his name.'

'Well, well,' said Pat, his curiosity aroused. 'What does he look like?'

'I haven't seen him, but their boy told me about him. He's tall and lanky and shabbily dressed.'

56

'You're a good little girl,' Pat announced as he picked up the anchor. 'Whereabouts is the Ile-Goulvan?'

'Beyond here. The best anchorage is at the foot of the cliff by a big rock sticking out like a jetty.'

Fredo had already started the outboard as Pat clambered aboard, smiling his thanks at the girl. The *Waikiki* roared away from the beach and vanished round the point. Lise stood and thought for a moment in the shade of the pine, then she made her way slowly back to the yellow house.

'Who was that?' her mother asked.

'A couple of visitors looking for a friend.'

'I expect they'll find him over at the Guidics'.'

'That's what I told them.'

Lise was beginning to feel sorry that she'd made it so easy for them to pick up the scent. Looking back on it, she suddenly realized that the crew of the *Waikiki* might not have been all they seemed and that there was something suspicious in the haste with which they had made off. She was wondering how to make good her mistake when, luckily, Madame Jégo quite unconsciously provided the excuse.

'Take the little punt and go over to Goulvan to say hullo to old Mamm Guidic. Uncle Job forgot to take our baskets back with him. You can collect half a gallon of milk and the week's vegetables while you're there.'

Lise approached the island where the coastline was low and green and the currents less strong than in the main channel. She propelled the punt skilfully, using the heavy oar over the stern. It surged ahead, the waves beating its flat bottom like a drum. To starboard a distant sound of lowing cattle, interrupted by the barking of Merlin, the Guidics' terrible four-footed cowman, came from Cow Island.

Further on, she crossed the path of a long string of

yachts sweeping down to the harbours of Locmariaquer and Port-Navalo or the open sea beyond. She hardly heard their laughter and shouts of encouragement. At all costs she had to keep her eyes open for the return of Fanch and his companion to warn them about these new visitors to the Ile-Goulvan. For all she knew, she might be able to stop them falling into some stupid trap.

The ebbtide was flowing strongly. Vainly Lise scanned the horizon for the *Petit-Emile*. She let the punt drift down on the Ile-Goulvan, neatly beaching it in Sow Cove. The *Waikiki* was already there, moored to the buoy. Not a soul was in sight and the silent island seemed deserted.

Hearing the sound of an outboard motor approaching the point, Mamm came out to take up her usual almost ceremonial stand by the gateway into the yard. She thought it was probably Monsieur Le Glohec in his launch or else the postman or the Jégos, so she was very surprised to see two complete strangers in a brand-new boat with sparkling chrome fittings. Secretively they disembarked, held a brief and muttered conference on the water's edge and then, to Mamm's astonishment, came running up the road swiftly and silently in their rubber-soled shoes.

It was only at the last minute that they saw her, dressed all in black, standing in the archway. Pat had had every intention of taking a strong line, but he was pulled up short by the old lady's presence and by her cold glance which seemed to say: 'I am the mistress and guardian of Goulvan.' Sheepishly they took off their caps. Mamm noticed that they were both of the same build, dressed alike, and, what is more, that each was the twin of the other in the sinister expression they wore. None the less a smile of welcome softened her stony look.

'What do you want?'

'We're looking for our old pal Benny Cosquer,' Pat said

cheerfully. 'Your neighbours' little girl told us the rat was lodging with you.'

He had said too much. Mamm knew at once that the two toughs were no friendly visitors inquiring for her guest.

'Benny's gone out for the day with my foster-son,' she told them firmly. 'You'd better come back at high tide tomorrow morning. It'll give me time to arrange lunch for you.'

'Where's his room?' Pat asked. 'I hope you've made him nice and comfortable. Benny isn't at all well, you know.'

He laughed. He was edging closer and closer to the poor old lady. Fredo stood in the background, his shifty eyes scanning the yard with its fig-trees and the garden stretching green beyond, framed by the girders of the water-tower. His impassive silence warned Mamm that he was the more dangerous of the two, and she cursed the absence of her brother, Job, working in the potato-patch at the other end of the island.

'Pardon,' said Pat, shoving her roughly aside. 'We'd like to have a look through his luggage to find something of ours. So now I come to think of it, it doesn't really matter if that rat Benny isn't there.'

They walked briskly along the front of the house kicking open the doors until at last they reached the guest-room. By the time Mamm got there they had torn the clothes off the bed, shifted all the furniture and emptied Benny's case. Clothing and packets of cigarettes were scattered around while the pair thumbed unsuccessfully through a handful of papers. Furiously angry, they now bore down upon Mamm.

'Where's the rest of the stuff?'

'Nowhere. The Ile-Goulvan's never been a place for thieves. But don't you worry, Fanch'll make you pay for all this.'

'Who's he?'

She cackled with laughter and her amusement unnerved the two men. Anxiously they peered outside, but there was nothing. The farm was still and silent. Then Fredo stepped behind the old lady and forced her gently but firmly into an armchair, to which he tied her wrists and ankles with strips of towel. She went on laughing.

'You alone here?' Pat snapped.

Mamm regained her breath and stared at the two men. They were from a world quite unknown to the islanders.

'We don't know the meaning of that word here,' she said. 'We have the sea all around us to guard us. You two are alone, not me.'

Her shrill laughter rang out again. They swung sharply round. There, filling the doorway, was the burly figure of Uncle Job standing fair and square on his bandy legs, his blue cap crammed down over his ears and a dog-end hanging from the corner of his mouth. He seemed as unconcerned as if he were hoeing potatoes, but the shot-gun under his arm was aimed unwaveringly at the sitting ducks who had flown over to the Ile-Goulvan.

'Untie the lady at once,' he growled, 'and stop fooling about. When you've done that you can lie flat on the bed and have a little snooze until your friend Benny comes back. And don't you try your tricks on me, I fought the war in the trenches of Vauquois. That's fifty years ago, I know, and ancient history as far as you're concerned, but you'll be making a very big mistake if you take me for a mug.'

An inquisitive little face peered round behind him. It was Lise, who now slipped into the room, and ignoring the intruders, set Mamm Guidic free. Then she took the old lady into the kitchen and bathed her forehead with vinegar.

'What a fool I was, Mamm! I sent those swine over to

60

you. It was a good thing Uncle Job saw me coming over in the punt. He came back to the farm to get my baskets ready and it didn't take him a minute to have his gun down off the hooks.'

The old lady's eyes were dark with anger.

'That doesn't matter, my girl. The sooner we get rid of this nasty business the better. Fanch will be back soon, with our lodger. Don't say a word, just let Benny come back to the farm. He can settle things with his friends. Whether he likes it or not he's leaving with them on their boat. I'm not having that sort of person in my house.'

At about eleven o'clock a red sail appeared to the north of the Ile-Goulvan, running down on the outfall from the River Noyalo. Around Langle, the tide was far out and the workers were swarming over the oyster-parks once more. Lise ran back to the yard to tell Mamm Guidic and to nod to Uncle Job on guard outside the guest-room.

From the very moment the *Petit-Emile* had turned for home, Benny had been cursing the way the tide-tables rigidly cut short his investigations.

'Whose fault's that?' Fanch had retorted. 'You should have been more careful noting your landmarks. The whole thing's so silly. You run aground slap bang in the middle of a marsh, you abandon ship without taking a fix on the exact place, and then, a couple of months later you're surprised you can't find it again!'

'And what if this boat had been lying there for a hundred years or more?' Benny suggested.

Fanch goggled. The wonders promised by this jump back in time took his breath away.

'In that case you'd better show me your map. I'd surely understand it better than you.'

'It's only been lent to me and I stand to lose a lot if I make the least slip.'

'You'll lose a lot more by not trusting me . . . What was the yacht called? Where was she from?'

But Benny turned angrily away. Meanwhile the green island had drawn nearer and Fanch, who had a keen pair of eyes, was the first to notice the glitter of the blue and white launch in Sow Bay.

'We've got visitors,' he announced. 'Are they for Mamm or you? We don't generally get luxury craft like that calling at Goulvan. Were you expecting anybody?'

'Me? No.'

Benny's face went pale beneath its tan and he stared tensely shorewards.

'Bear away from the cove,' he ordered a moment later. 'Take her in by the pine-trees. My doctor told me to avoid excitement in my state, and I don't want to run into any upsets.'

Fanch obeyed unquestioningly. Once more he was master of the *Petit-Emile,* but his passenger held the clue to a splendid adventure which unwound from island to island across the shifting tides of the Little Sea. They needed one another to unravel the mystery, the one for its own sake, the other for the sake of what it would bring him, and this need made them stick like burrs.

There was still two foot of water on the other side of the pines. Fanch came in by the cow-track which wound up through the bushes and across the heath. Benny disembarked first, taking the anchor which he fixed firmly in the damp sand.

'Now it's all arranged, isn't it? You won't let me down at the last minute, will you?'

'We'll get off at half tide,' Fanch assured him. 'It'll take us up there by sunset, so we'll have two full hours of daylight to cruise round between Saint-Goustan and Noyalo.'

He furled the sail and climbed overboard. Benny was still gloomy and distrustful.

'You go first and have a good look at these visitors. I won't put in an appearance at the farm until the coast's clear.'

'I expect they're only harmless campers. We get quite a lot of them because of the fresh water. Mamm gives them the run of the place and we never have any trouble from them.'

'You little fool!' Benny growled. 'That's just the set-up I'm most afraid of at the moment.'

Silently and in single file they came up the sunken track to pause for a moment behind the thick hedge of tamarisks on the south side of the yard. Before venturing further, Fanch pulled the branches aside. The farm lay silent in the bright sunlight. All seemed normal. Mamm was pottering about the kitchen garden, while Uncle Job sat on a chair facing the guest-room with his back to them. Nobody else was about.

'Seems all right,' he whispered.

It was only when they both pushed through the hedge that Fanch noticed Lise standing motionless in the shade of the fig-trees, facing the gateway. He gave a low whistle to attract her attention. She swung round wide-eyed and gave him a strange look, but said nothing.

'You came over in that blue and white outboard?' Fanch called to her and laughed.

He came nearer, the lodger lagging behind and peering this way and that, when suddenly Uncle Job jumped up from his chair to disclose the shot-gun which had been nestling between his knees.

'You can come out now!' he shouted through the door. 'Your dear old pal's just turned up. You grab him by the scruff of the neck and clear out, the lot of you – the Ile-Goulvan's not a pirates' rest home!'

As the two toughs came charging out of their cell like mad bulls, Benny made a panic-stricken dash for the hedge. There was quite a scuffle in the tamarisks before the pair finally caught him. Hideous groans announced his capture, and at length the couple reappeared, fisting their prisoner in front of them. Blood was streaming down Benny's face and his sweat-shirt hung in tatters, revealing his pigeon chest. As they passed, Uncle Job chucked the small suitcase at them. Pat caught it.

'The three hundred francs for his board and lodging are in an envelope. The old lady won't touch stolen money ... Now get out of it quick, and don't you ever come back to the Ile-Goulvan!'

Fanch, who had been standing beside Lise in the shade of the fig-trees, now began to reproach himself bitterly for having betrayed his comrade. He viewed Benny as a very shady character, but Benny held the clue to a mystery and the hints he had thrown out had made Fanch determined to solve it.

'It wouldn't have taken much more for that gun to go off in my hands!' Uncle Job said as he came back. 'Would you credit it, those swine had the nerve to set hands on old Mamm?'

The boy caught them up at the water's edge, a few feet from the *Waikiki*. Pat had just slung Benny aboard and Fredo was loosing the moorings, when behind them they heard a strange whistling sound like a scythe or a wind-vane. It was Fanch, running at full tilt, whirling an oar above his head. They turned, but had no time to defend themselves. Pat caught the first blow across the back of the neck and fell face downwards into the mud. Fredo dodged the second, but the third got him right in the guts and laid him alongside his partner. Neither could get up until he had had his share of the blows which Fanch dealt turn and turn about to relieve his all-consuming anger. Benny had staggered to his feet in the boat and laughed until the tears poured down his cheeks.

64

'Well done, son! I was beginning to think you'd let me down. Here, give me a hand!'

But Fanch thrust his outstretched arm aside. The other two got shakily to their feet and tumbled into the boat. Fredo could not see for the blood in his eyes. He groped for the starter and the *Waikiki* rocketed out to sea, rapidly vanishing behind Sow Rock.

Fanch wept with rage as he walked back to the farm. The punishment he had inflicted on the thugs seemed paltry. Mamm Guidic had given him a home; she had tended him in sickness; she had rescued him from the horrors of the orphanage, and her person was sacred. When he had been younger, he had fought like a wildcat for her, in Uncle Job's absence, against wandering drunks, chicken-stealers from Le Bono or the suburbs of Vannes, and roughs in speedboats who caused trouble to impress their girls.

'Well, you didn't use a feather-duster on them,' Uncle Job remarked as he took the oar from him. 'I don't know if Benny'll miss Mamm's cooking, but the other two won't forget their little trip to Goulvan in a hurry.'

Mamm Guidic came through the archway and the grief in her eyes hurt Fanch.

'Benny wasn't all that bad,' she said sadly. 'Why did they hit him?'

Fanch rubbed his eyes. He still felt muzzy.

'From what I can make out,' he said slowly, 'they either lost or scuttled a luxury yacht up the River Noyalo. It must have been a darned fine boat, worth a lot, too. This was all two or three months ago, or maybe even longer. Their trouble is they can't find the place again. When Benny saw the *Petit-Emile,* he thought it was the dinghy from this yacht, and that's how it all started.'

Mamm would have no truck with stolen goods and she looked sharply at Fanch.

'Then you'll strip her right away and sink her in the channel,' she said coldly. 'The flood tide tonight may make a present of her to some other fool. I'm not having any more of this nonsense here ... Where's your old boat?'

'I lent her to some kids over at Saint-Arzhel. Nephews of Monsieur Le Glohec.'

'Uncle can take you over tomorrow morning on the punt and you can get her back. Is that a promise?'

Fanch agreed wholeheartedly, with Lise's smile to soften the dreadful blow. Mamm's expression changed at once and she ruffled his hair.

'Wake up, lad! It's all been a bad dream.'

'Whew!' Fanch cheered up. 'It wasn't so bad in parts.'

4

The Castaway on La Teigne

FIRST Fanch carefully unstepped the mast and laid it across the thwarts, and then Lise helped him carry it up the beach well above the high-water mark. It took them several trips to remove the new sail, the bottom-boards which had come from the original *Petit-Emile,* the rudder and tiller, the bait-tin, the anchor, the lines and a haversack full of the odds and ends which accumulate in any boat, no matter what size she is. Soon all that was left was the black hull. Stripped as she was, the boat still bobbed like a living thing on the waves and Fanch found it hard to hide the misery he felt.

'Good, that's that!' he told Lise. 'I'll keep one oar and you can take it aboard at the last moment. Put the lines and the packet of oakum with the rest of the stuff. I'll have a last look at her and then we can push off. Don't forget your baskets.'

In the distance the mudflats sparkled in the blazing midday sun. The horizon was lost in the heat-haze. Lise went up the beach with her load and vanished for a moment in the shadows of the pines which lined the creek. Fanch inspected the boat for the last time, peering under the thwarts and gunwale. Nothing remained; the hull was stripped and derelict. He sat down wearily with his back against the stempost in exactly the same attitude adopted by the bad-tempered Benny during the two hours of their return trip that morning.

As he was settling himself, his hand chanced to brush against the edge of a piece of paper slipped between one

68

of the ribs and the planking of the bows. Curious, Fanch got down on all fours in the bottom of the boat and with the blade of his knife gently eased the piece of paper out of the crack. As he withdrew it, it unfolded slightly. Lise came across the damp sand to watch over his shoulder.

'Found something?'

Fanch did not stir.

'It's Benny's map. He must have been frightened that the others were on his track and tried to hide it, so as to keep one jump ahead of them.'

'Put it back where you found it. Let it go down with the boat. That'll be the best for everyone.'

Lise loaded the baskets and the churn of milk aboard the punt and then got in herself.

'You go first and keep well in sight,' Fanch told her, forcing a laugh. 'I don't want to be all alone when the *Petit-Emile* goes under.'

Clear of Sow Rock, the tide took them swiftly past the cliffs. At first they chatted as they sculled side by side.

'Where are you going to scuttle her?' Lise asked. 'There's no point going miles to do it.'

'I reckon to put her down between the two islands where no one can see us from the mainland.'

'You should have ballasted her with rocks.'

'And find her washed up on your foreshore a couple of days after? Do you think I'm mad? ... No, the lighter she is the further the tide'll take her and the faster we'll be rid of her.'

Now they had reached the southerly tip of the Ile-Goulvan. All around them the weed-fringed mudbanks were emerging from the water and joining to form a shimmering foreshore, seamed by gullies feeding the main channel.

Suddenly Fanch stopped sculling.

'Come alongside!' he called to Lise. 'I want you to take

my oar. And then try to stick as close as you can, I shan't abandon ship until the very end.'

He bent down in the stern to loosen the bung. It was very stiff and squeaked like the tap of a wine-cask, but at last a sharp tap knocked it out and the water came spurting in. Fanch sat back on the thwart and almost immediately the water was up to his ankles. He did not move, fixedly watching the sea slowly taking back its own. Gradually the boat grew sluggish and unstable.

'Coming?' Lise asked.

'Not yet. I'll wait till the water's up to her gunwales, just to make sure. Otherwise she could turn over with a pocket of air still in the hull and people might see her floating down to Port-Navalo like a whale. As she carries a well-known name on her stern, I'd be called a wrecker on top of everything else!'

When the water was up to his knees, he stepped carefully on to the thwart and from there into Lise's punt. She had to scull hard to get clear of the sinking boat. It seemed to follow them, turning slowly in their wake, but soon all that could be seen were the gunwales and the stempost, and then, with a slight shudder, the shadowy shape of the *Petit-Emile* disappeared into the depths.

'Good-bye, good luck and good riddance!' Fanch called, raising his arm. He looked wretched though, and this upset Lise.

'Forget her. Maybe the sea'll wash up another for you, one without her bad reputation.'

'I'll make more inquiries before I take over another,' Fanch grunted.

During the scuttling operation the bottom of his shorts had got wet. He squeezed them out and removed a soggy piece of paper from one of the pockets.

'Goodness! I'd forgotten about the map ... What did we say we'd do with it?'

70

He was all ready to tear it into small pieces and send it after the sunken dinghy.

'What does it show?' Lise asked.

'A bit of coastline with the bearings in red. But it's nothing like anything round here, I'm sure of that . . . Here, you take a look at it.'

The roughly-drawn map meant much less to them than the dark shadow of the *Petit-Emile* gradually disappearing into the swirling tide. Fanch was still far too upset by the whole business to care about the scrap of paper.

'Shall I chuck it away?'

Lise hesitated a moment. What could be wrong in keeping it?

'You hold on to it,' she said. 'You never know, someone a bit more honest than Benny and a bit sharper than we are might find it handy one day.'

It was a blazing hot day, but it was the last low tide that was most useful, and on the Ile-Hervé they used every minute of it in the oyster-parks. Monsieur Jégo took his workmen home in the big punt with the outboard motor, finishing the trip at the Ile-Goulvan, where he landed an utterly exhausted Fanch.

'I'm ready to drop,' the boy admitted, as he came ashore in Sow Bay.

'That's your fault. Why did you have to get up so early this morning? The islands aren't going to fly away like a flock of seagulls. You've got the whole of your life in front of you to go tacking between the estuaries at Vannes and Le Bono. Those spoiled brats of Larmor-Baden pick up just as much in their plywood tubs during the holidays.'

'Ah!' Fanch sighed. 'It's not the same at all. A good thing if the Little Sea is big enough for them.'

'Well then, what do you want?'

'To get out to the open sea, way beyond Port-Navalo.'

'Oh, come on, it's not so bad for you with the Guidics. What more do you want?'

Fanch pointed to the empty beach and the mooring buoy dancing on the waves.

'My boat. I can't bear being without it. For the last two or three hours I've felt as though my leg has been cut off.'

'You'll have it back when you go over to Saint-Arzhel tomorrow morning,' Monsieur Jégo called to him as he turned the punt. 'A good old boat never forgets its skipper.'

Fanch walked up to the farm feeling very sorry for himself. There was no one there to welcome him. Uncle Job was still over on Cow Island, Mamm was somewhere around looking after the rabbits and the fowls, and the lodger they had thrown out was probably at that very moment being cuffed from island to island under a prolonged third-degree from his two kidnappers. Fanch sat down at the table, laid his head on his arms and fell fast asleep. He only woke up when a steaming bowl of soup was set before him. It was nearly dark by now, but no seabreeze relieved the oppressive atmosphere. The old couple looked at him oddly.

'Eat your supper and hurry up to bed,' said Uncle Job. 'I'll wake you first thing in the morning. We'll have twenty crates of vegetables to load aboard, the chickens, a dozen rabbits and the two calves Monsieur Lévenez ordered this morning for the hotels. The season's starting. We've got to be at Sarzeau market in good time and we'll have to take our Noah's Ark over to Cow Island first of all.'

Fanch went back to sleep in his little room. He woke to find the moonlight streaming in on him. The waters of the gulf were silvered over and the wavelets whispered like the broad seas on a fine summer's night. Fanch made no sound as he got up, slipped on a pair of sandals and went down to the kitchen. The clock struck the half-hour after midnight. Outside the fig-trees and the grass in the yard

72

were blue-black in the frosty light. All was quiet in the farm and outbuildings and only Uncle Job's full-throated snores, escaping from a half-open window, disturbed the peace of the night.

Fanch went under the arch and down the road to Sow Bay. The tide had already uncovered the rocks which stood out in the chalky radiance of the moon. On the distant, scarcely visible coast of Séné tiny red and yellow lights winked dimly through the ground-haze. Fanch scrambled up the point. From there he could see Arz and the Isle-aux-Moines, the two big islands merged in the distance like one enormous dazzling ice-floe across the water. This was far too good a night to waste in anything so dull as sleep. Fanch began to walk along the top of the cliffs while the tide washed the shore with a ceaseless murmur.

Fanch walked on, listening to the gossip of the waves, only to stop once more, his ears pricked. From the far distant direction of the Ile-d'Hur the silence was broken by a despairing cry which mingled with the music of the waves. Fanch changed course and cut across the heath. Here the sound of the waves grew fainter and fainter, but he could hear the cry grow suddenly more clear. Two miles, or even less, from the Ile-Goulvan, someone was in trouble.

In splendid isolation, La Teigne stood in the centre of the channel, its presence marked by a stone pillar ringed in red and white paint. Exceptionally high tides left only the tip of this beacon visible, but in normal conditions there would be about eight by ten feet of the hump-backed reef – crowned by bracken and dry marram-grass, roughly the size of a small room – above high water mark. Benny, however, was in no mood to make the best of what little comfort there was, and had since dusk been vainly shouting to attract the attention of people ashore. The nearest were

73

these who lived on the farms on the Ile-d'Hur, nearly two miles away to the south, but there was small chance of the yells of the castaway disturbing their sleep.

As the moon rose, it cast a magnificent light upon the water, making the empty sleeping sea appear even more vast. There was not a boat in sight, the lights in the coastal villages had gone out and there was only the fleeting flash on the horizon from the lighthouses at Quiberon and Belle-Ile or the headlamps of the occasional late car on the Sarzeau road.

Benny rested a moment and then resumed the round of his prison, shouting curses to all points of the compass. In his rage he never even noticed the little punt coming down the channel, a tiny black dot on the waters silvered by the moon. Fanch approached La Teigne cross-current, leaped agilely on to the rock and bent down to moor the punt. As he stood up, he found himself face to face with a nightmare figure. Benny gave a moan and began babbling like an old woman.

'F–F–Fanch, is it really you? W–W–Where have you sprung from? P–P–Please don't leave me here.'

The boy could hardly recognize his fellow-sailor of the morning. Benny's clothes were torn and the blood which caked his bruised and swollen face made it look almost black in the moonlight.

'Did your mates leave you like this . . . What happened?'

'When we left you, Pat and Fredo dragged me off to the Seven Marshes . . . you can guess why. We paddled about in the mud for hours and didn't find a thing. On their way back, they landed me on this rock and gave me a real beating-up. You can see the results, I'm half dead; I can only see out of one eye and those swine knocked four or five of my teeth out – and all to get the map.'

'And did you give it them?' Fanch asked innocently.

Benny was quite brazen.

74

'I'd hidden it so well that the fools had to rip my clothes to shreds before they found it . . . you'll never guess where . . . stuck on to the sole of my shoe with a piece of Sellotape. But don't think they were any gentler now they'd won. They made off like a couple of murderers, leaving poor Benny on this wretched rock to suffer torments ever since it got dark.'

'What are you going to do?'

'I shan't give up the chase. The map they grabbed off me won't get them very far, and that leaves me a chance. But if I'm to beat them at their game, Fanch, I'll have to be able to rely on you.'

A few hours earlier this plea would have got him nowhere. The man really seemed hopeless, but his pitiful state undermined Fanch's best resolutions, and Fanch again found himself drawn into the secret complicity which had bound them together in the morning mist.

'Of course I'll take you off here. The first thing we've got to do is patch you up a bit, you don't even look human. And then I'll try and find somewhere for you to sleep. You won't get into a hotel looking like that . . . Where do you want to go?'

'I'm a real tramp now! Those swine stripped me of every penny I had and left me for dead. It's lucky I'm pretty tough. Know what we'll do? Help me aboard the punt and get me back to the farm as quick as you can. I shan't be sorry to be back in your guest-room. A few days' rest will put me back on my feet. The old lady's a good old soul, she'll give me credit and I'll see she gets her money back – and a good bit more on top of it.'

'You'll never set foot on the Ile-Goulvan again,' Fanch said very firmly. 'I'd like to help you but I'm not doing anything Mamm wouldn't like . . . And don't try to bully me into it, or I'll leave you here. You could have a little snooze while you wait for the next boat to show up. She'd

probably be the *Bombard,* the coastguard cutter. But don't worry, the crew are good at first-aid.'

Benny sat back with a groan.

'Just get me away quick, or I'll die.'

Fanch helped him down to the punt and settled his lanky form on the bottom boards with his head pillowed on his suitcase. The tide soon took them clear of La Teigne.

'All I can do for you at the moment,' said Fanch, 'is to land you on Cow Island. It's as good a place as any and nobody will bother you there. There's plenty of fresh water in the tank. The cowshed's falling to pieces, but you'll find a cosy corner to sleep in, and I'll come over every other day to bring you some food. Uncle Job won't worry you; you can see him coming from miles away and you'll have plenty of time to hide.'

Benny seemed to lose consciousness for a moment. All the same, whenever Fanch glanced towards the bows he caught the glint of an eye. The man was tough. Despite the beating he had taken, his mind and its grasp of the situation were unimpaired. The punt was labouring along the Ile-Hervé, when he raised himself on one elbow.

'You're a good lad, Fanch. If it hadn't been for you, the morning tide would have taken me out past Port-Navalo, and I'd have been crabs' meat. So much for me! Do you think anyone would care if I disappeared? Not a soul – not even my landlady's cat! But that's what happens to lone-wolves who chase adventure . . .'

Fanch had his back to Benny as he sculled over the stern.

'They could hear you bellowing from miles away,' he answered unemotionally. 'No one came to take you off La Teigne sooner because folk round the Little Sea have had a hot and tiring day. Everyone on the islands was fast asleep by nine o'clock . . . I don't suppose you believe in anything, but, by golly, Our Lady of Auray certainly woke me up in the nick of time, and, thank goodness, the channel was as bright as day. I sculled like mad when I heard you cursing on the reef.'

'How's the *Petit-Emile*?' Benny asked sleepily. 'I hope you've got her firmly moored in Sow Bay.'

'I scuttled her in the channel this morning,' Fanch answered with a show of unconcern. 'About time too! You can't hang on to something which brings you so much trouble. Anyway, that's what you'd have wanted me to do yourself.'

Benny stood up in the punt.

'You little fool!' he yelled. 'Where is she?'

'You can still go and look for her. If you ask me, the boat probably split at about four o'clock when she was carried against the Mare's Nose. The ebb tide runs at about twelve knots around there and if the next flood tide brings you anything back, it won't be more than match-wood!'

Benny slumped back in the bottom, quite overcome by the news, and did not utter another word until the punt grounded on the sand. The tide was right out. Fanch had to heave him up the beach and haul him across the meadow where Mamm Guidic's Friesians slept in a ring round their guard. The dog stood up in the moonlight and growled and showed his teeth until he heard a friendly voice. Then he quietened and came over to lick his young master's hand and sniff in a friendly fashion at the stranger.

'You'll get on all right together.' Fanch laughed. 'Merlin's a lone-wolf too. Hold up! We're nearly there.'

They could see the stars through the gaping roof of the cowshed. Fanch groped for the door of the warm and dusty fodder-store in which he had so often slept as a cowboy. Benny gave a sigh of relief as he stretched his battered frame on a pile of kelp.

'I'll draw two buckets of fresh water. Have a good drink and wash your face. You don't look exactly handsome. I'll go across to Goulvan to get you some food and bedding.

78

It'll soon be daylight and then the tide'll be even lower. If you feel strong enough you can walk over to the Ile Tascon without getting your feet wet. From there you can get across to the oyster-parks at Saint-Arzhel, and that would be the best thing you could do, as far as all of us are concerned.'

An hour later Benny was fast asleep and snoring in the close darkness. The dog had snuggled up against him and seemed glad of his company. Fanch threw a tattered blanket over him and left a haversack with some food within easy reach. All was going well. Doubtless one dose of solitude had been enough, and when the castaway of La Teigne awoke he would be in a hurry to get on his way.

When Fanch returned to Goulvan it was too late to go back to bed, for the stars were fading in the grey light of dawn. Uncle Job had just got up and was re-heating the coffee in the dark of the kitchen.

'What have you been up to this time, son? I've just been to your room and your bed was cold.'

Fanch told the exact truth when he said, 'I've just hauled the first eight crates down to the cove.'

'I don't know what's got into you in the last day or so,' Uncle Job went on. 'Now if you ever see either of those two toughs again, you just steer clear of them and come back and let me know.'

They worked in silence until sunrise, only bringing down the fowls and rabbits, which Mamm Guidic had put into their cages, at the last moment. The heavily-laden punt chugged up the cross-channel which took the outflow from Saint-Arzhel. The closer they got to Cow Island the greater grew Fanch's fear of a scarecrow figure emerging from the cowshed to greet them. But all was quiet and only Merlin came bounding through the long grass to round up the herd. It took them a good hour to finish the milking and stack the churns on the punt. Leaving Uncle

Job to play cow-boy with the two recalcitrant calves, Fanch next went to inspect the cowshed. Hoping to find the fodder-store empty, he kicked open the door.

Unfortunately, there was Benny, lying flat on his back, his hands crossed under the back of his head, a cigarette in his mouth and a blissful expression on his face. He had washed his face and the swellings had gone down noticeably while he had been asleep. However, his black eye had gone a fearful shade of purple and there was nothing attractive about his gap-toothed smile.

'Fanch, my dear boy,' he said coolly. 'I think my best course is to take up residence on Cow Island. In the first place Pat and Fredo will never come this far to look for me, and then it will be so easy for us to keep in touch, and finally, in case of need, I have a line of retreat to the mainland. What do you think of that, now?'

Fanch showed his dislike of the whole scheme.

'Don't get it into your head I'm coming over with your breakfast, dinner and supper three times a day! I'm not stripping the larder of Goulvan to fatten a good-for-nothing like you. If you're really hungry, join our cattle in a good meal of grass! But you'd better leave here fast, man, or Uncle Job's going to think something's up and then the police from Sarzeau'll come over and pick you up.'

'Give me a couple of days at least,' Benny begged him. 'I feel as weak as a kitten and my nose hasn't stopped bleeding yet. Do you think anyone'ld let me on a bus looking like this?'

'All right, two days then, and not a minute more!' Fanch said as he shut the door.

'Wait a minute, you idiot!'

Benny sat up and produced some money from his tatters.

'I thought your pals had cleaned you out,' Fanch said coldly.

'I wasn't born yesterday!' Benny laughed. 'I hid five thousand francs in the lining of my sponge-bag. I use it as a wallet when I'm on a job . . . Anyway, here's three hundred francs. Be a good boy and buy some clothes to fit me. Something hardwearing and inconspicuous. If I'm dressed like the local people, no one will take any notice of me. Now, listen hard! I've been thinking things over, Fanch, and if it comes to it, I don't really need that map to explore the River Noyalo. If you'll be my guide, that'll be enough. With my memory and your local knowledge, sooner or later we'll find what we're looking for. But we're not going to make that long trip astride one of Mamm Guidic's rabbit-hutches, so the big question at the moment is, where are we going to get a boat?'

His spirits had risen again, his eyes were bright and cheerful, and Fanch yielded once more to the mysterious attraction which this odd character held for him.

'We'll get one from Saint Arzhel,' he answered. 'I'm just going over to recover the *Petit-Emile*, the old one that is, the one you don't know. She should be just big enough to take the pair of us.'

It was six in the morning. Monsieur Le Glohec had not failed to keep the regular rendezvous and was waiting on the quayside in his old van. Twice a week he would pick up his old friend Job Guidic with a load and take them to Sarzeau. They had very little trouble in trans-shipping their cargo, except for the two calves – and these bellowed so loudly that they must have woken the entire village.

When all the rest were safely ashore, Fanch unloaded the gear for the *Petit-Emile*. Neatly bundled, it lay amid the lobster-pots on the edge of the wharf.

'I don't know how the kids have treated your boat,' Monsieur Le Glohec called to him just before he drove off. 'It should be high and dry on the little beach at La Senne, just below the Hotel Armoric. If you need a hand getting her afloat, you go and haul those idle young ruffians out of bed. My niece'll give you some breakfast.'

'Leave the punt moored to the wharf and get back to Goulvan as quickly as you can,' added Uncle Job. 'With all these villains knocking around the islands, I don't want Mamm left on her own for too long at a time.'

They were off at last. The village was only just awake in the morning light which gilded the white houses in front of Fanch. As ever, he set foot on the mainland with some caution. For the moment, the only living thing in sight was the cat curled up on the doorstep of Monsieur Guéguen's baker's shop. But beyond the line of elms to starboard twinkled the slate roof of the village school, and behind its dusty windows Blackbeard could well be on the prowl.

Fanch went far out of his way to avoid the danger zone, only to run slap into the parish priest, who chanced to be walking slowly back from church reading his breviary. Fanch knew quite well that priest and schoolmaster might work hand-in-glove to bring him back into the fold. With bated breath he tiptoed away. The other had not raised his eyes, but he hadn't missed Fanch.

'Hi!' the priest called cheerfully. 'Aren't we on speaking terms?'

Fanch turned, his heart sinking.

'I didn't want to interrupt you while you were reading your office, father,' he said, with cunning. 'Good morning, father.'

There was a beaming smile on the priest's round red face. Fanch was not a model parishioner, but then the tides are not always right for Sunday mass and islanders have a right to some dispensations.

'It must be two or three weeks since I last saw you here. What have you been up to on that island of yours?'

Fanch hung his head and tried to look as weary as he could.

'I've got almost more on my plate than I can manage, helping Mamm and Uncle and the Jégos.'

'Thank the Lord Mamm Guidic has brought you up a good Christian. All the same, you should make a little effort to get to church and to school. It's not a very good thing at your age to live such a lonely life.'

'Monsieur Cogan can't teach me any more,' Fanch said sulkily.

'That may be, but he isn't particularly happy when his brightest pupil leaves him in the lurch. What's got you up so early this morning? I can't imagine anyone coming this way just to gather shrimps and winkles on some forsaken mudbank.'

Silence. Fanch was heartily regretting this unwelcome meeting and trying to think of an excuse to get away. He decided to come out into the open.

'Will you tell him you've seen me in Saint-Arzhel?'

'I'm not a spy,' the parish priest retorted sharply. 'Monsieur Cogan won't need my help when the time comes to get his hands on you . . . Ah-ha!'

His laugh was more of a warning than a threat, and once he had gone Fanch looked anxiously around. The quayside and the roads leading down to the harbour were starting to come to life, but there was something reassuring about the morning bustle. If Blackbeard were hiding in some dark corner, the boy would at once be given the alarm by his allies – the fishermen and the owners of the waterside shops.

Off he ran and did not stop until he had reached the beach below the hotel. The *Petit-Emile* was there all right, drawn up on the sand between two fishing-boats, a few yards from a tidal inlet. Fanch felt a wave of joy flood over him at the sight of her trim and sturdy lines. The young wizard of the Little Sea had magicked her out of Monsieur Riou's spare time. The old man of Langle had built her and Fanch had watched her slowly take shape, timber by timber, in the boatyard, while the patriarch poured out a wonderful flow of reminiscence of his days under sail on a Cape Horner, and in a lower voice complained of the bitterness of ageing so fast.

5

The Wreck of the *Berenice*

THE Hotel Armoric stood at the far end of the sea front,
shut off from the village by a line of screening pines. The
coast road petered out into a sandy track among the gorse
and dunes overlooking the beach, and it was here that Pat
and Fredo had been lying up since sunrise, watching
through their binoculars the occasional craft making for
Saint-Arzhel.

Thus they had been able to follow the punt as it put off
from the Ile-Goulvan; they had watched the boat anchor
for some considerable time at Cow Island and then come
puttering up the fairway to the wharf. They could not see
her tie up and unload her cargo because the pier was in
the way, but they heard the despairing bellows of the
calves clearly enough.

A little later the boy had appeared along the still-empty
road. Instead of continuing along the track through the
dunes, which would have suited the watchers so admirably,
he suddenly cut off and went running down the beach to
the low-water mark.

Pat delivered a mumbled running-commentary, as he
watched his prey, the binoculars glued to his eyes.

'That black boat's the thing that interests him at the
moment. And what's more, it looks awfully like the one we
saw coming out of the mouth of the River Noyalo . . . If
you ask me, Fredo, the map doesn't matter very much.
It's quite likely Benny has destroyed it, once the kid's
shown him the lie of the land. We knocked him pretty silly
that night. He tried to pull us off the track with a load of

nonsense, but he couldn't help spilling a thing or two in the state he was in. If you ask me, that kid knows something and he's hoping to get his cut, and it won't be chicken-feed either. And even if he doesn't know he's quite a rival. He's the only one who can take a boat right up the backwaters of the Noyalo. We've got to keep him shadowed and that means one eye all the time on the Ile-Goulvan and the other on that red sail of his which cuts through the water almost as fast as the *Waikiki*.'

Fredo was impatient.

'Oh, shut up! All your bright theories don't get us a step nearer the *Berenice*. Time's running out, and we've got to work with the tides. I say we'd better grab the boy and get him on the job. If he won't help, a couple of good thumps'll soon make him change his mind.'

'Don't forget the way he caught you with that oar!' Pat sniggered and lowered the binoculars. 'All right, you go and talk to him, then – I'm staying here.'

Fanch could not see the blue and white hull of the *Waikiki*, lurking like a shark behind a sandbank. The tide was right out, the pool of water it had left behind on the beach had only one outlet to the main channel and it was in any case some distance from the harbour. Fanch looked at the *Petit-Emile* for a moment, thinking.

Fifty yards away he was fiercely observed from the top of the dune.

'Made up your mind, big boy?' hissed Pat.

Fredo slowly rose to his feet amid the gorse bushes, but the boy was already walking towards the harbour, following the line of seaweed left by the high tide. The other two stayed in hiding and argued on. Ten minutes later Fanch returned with the mast and the oars for the *Petit-Emile* balanced on his right shoulder.

A light breeze which scarcely ruffled the open waters of the gulf had sprung up. Fanch had a hard job to manhandle the boat as far as the channel, but stepping the mast was a different story. He was beginning to think he would never manage it on his own, when two holiday-makers came strolling down from the dunes, their hands in the pockets of their shorts.

'Want a hand?' Fredo's voice was friendly.

Fanch's eyes remained cold and watchful as he looked up at them. He tried to get his hands on an oar without their noticing.

'Do you think I'm crazy? I can guess the sort of help you'll give me. We've met before, you know. I was the one who tickled your ribs the other evening on the beach of the Ile-Goulvan.'

Pat roared with laughter.

'Oh, that was just a little misunderstanding. Take a look at us, we're all right you'll find us a bit more generous than your grandmother's lodger.'

'Benny's no good!' Fredo added. 'A down-and-out who's shoved his nose into our affairs.'

The boy was getting ready to run, so they moved apart to hem him in.

'You're a couple of thugs!' Fanch muttered. 'Benny's not far away and he's waiting to pay you back for what you did to him. When he does, you'll find me there to help him.'

The two men were all keyed up for action as Fanch got ready to run. All three then were lined up for the start. Suddenly Fanch broke away, head down, arms pumping. He won the race to the crest of the dune, lashed out like a young mule and caught Fredo full in the teeth, sending him tumbling and yelling backwards on his companion. The two toughs broke into a flood of curses.

'We'll get our own back, don't worry. That boat of yours will make fine firewood!'

Fanch scowled down at them.

'Go and try it then. I'm off to the harbour and I'll soon

be back with a dozen good tough friends. Then we'll see who'll laugh.'

He went leaping off towards the hotel, only to fall straight into the clutching arms of Blackbeard. The schoolmaster stepped out of the bushes to take the full impetus of the boy's flight and both fell crashing to the sand. Fanch

was up again at once, but Monsieur Cogan caught him round the legs and brought him down once more.

'Got you this time!'

'Let me go!' Fanch yelled, struggling with all his might.

For a few minutes there was a wild topsy-turvy scrimmage and then Fanch gave up the fight.

'This is the happiest day for me in the whole school year!' Blackbeard announced as he released his iron grip.

'If I hadn't been up all night,' Fanch sighed bitterly, 'I'd have had you chasing me full tilt round the village – and I'd have got away over the cemetery wall, like I did last time.'

Monsieur Cogan put out his hand and pulled him so roughly to his feet that they found themselves quite literally face to face. They both started to laugh.

'The silly thing,' Monsieur Cogan admitted, 'is that the only reason I was on the dunes was to keep an eye on those two clowns . . . but now I've got you, I'm going to keep you. There's a nice little room with bars across the windows waiting for you back at the school. You've all summer in front of you to swot up for the entrance exam to the High School at Lorient.'

Fanch shook his head.

'The Merchant Service can learn to do without me.' He made his position quite clear. 'I'm staying where I am on the Ile-Goulvan. I'd rather spend the rest of my life looking after the cows.'

Monsieur Cogan was not so imperceptive as to take the boast at its face value.

'Come off it, Fanch!' he said seriously. 'That's just playing. All the things which give you a kick are kids' stuff. But you're not a kid any more, you've got your future right in front of you. It's time you started to grow up and make your plans for the time when you'll be a man. You've got to break out of this little world of yours, because the older you grow the more cramping you're going to find it. . . Mamm Guidic knows this perfectly well and she knows she only holds you now by a thread. Sooner or later that thread's going to snap, Fanch, and it won't be so hard for the old lady if something beyond her control or yours snaps it. I'm the man who's got to do it and I don't like it one little bit. But do you think I'd go to all this trouble over someone I didn't think worth it?'

Fanch was touched to find how much the schoolmaster really cared, when the boy had for so long regarded him as unfeeling and unkind. But far from his school and without his sinister grey jacket, Monsieur Cogan was the best of good fellows, and in his blue guernsey and old canvas slacks he fitted well into the fishing community of the harbour. The fringe of black hair round his jaw which had earned him his nickname was not even out of place. This affectation underlined a strain in the ancestry of the islanders which lent many of them a certain physical distinction – five hundred years earlier, the intrepid Spanish mariners had called at the islands on their way to Vannes.

Fanch took a deep breath, filling his lungs with the good sea air. He let his gaze wander to the fresh sunlit horizon and the innumerable islands studding the pale blue sea. The thought of giving up his childhood's paradise brought tears to his eyes.

'I know you're right,' he murmured, 'but I don't want to lose it all.'

With weary resignation Monsieur Cogan let his hand drop from the boy's shoulder, as though he were giving up the attempt. He, too, was beginning to feel that there was something noble about Fanch's devotion to his native soil, and that it would be wicked to stifle it, even from the best of motives. Fanch turned away from the beach.

From the steep gully of sand through which the deep water channel flowed there came an angry roar. The blue-and-white hulled *Waikiki* leapt out of hiding, heading straight for the distant shores of the Isle-d'Arz, and was soon lost in the blinding glare of the gulf.

Miserably Fanch counted his last seconds of happiness slipping away, marking out of the corner of his eye the distance between himself and the *Petit-Emile*. As he thought over what he had just heard and only half understood, he realized that to break and run for it now would lower him beyond redemption in the other's eyes.

In gloomy silence Monsieur Cogan did nothing to restrain the boy as Fanch strolled unhurriedly down the slope of the dune and crossed the beach at the same lazy pace. He was making for the boat with the black hull mirrored in the waters of the channel, and when he got to her he looked back at Blackbeard with a broad grin on his face.

'I was just rigging her,' he called cheerfully. 'You wouldn't like to give me a hand, would you?'

He, too, felt it was only polite to leave the decision to the schoolmaster. Without another thought Monsieur Cogan came down on to the beach. It did not take them long to collect the tackle and refit the boat, for Blackbeard proved to be an expert, stepping the mast at the very first attempt. Fanch hoisted the sail and they pushed her out. The *Petit-Emile* floated free, dancing trimly and asking to be sailed. Monsieur Cogan took the invitation and threw his sandals over the side.

'Listen, Fanch,' he said cheerily, before hoisting himself aboard. 'We could come to an arrangement, you know. The little room with barred windows is only a joke, so let's forget it. But you really ought to try to settle down to a little work. Would it be too much to set aside part of your spare time for study? Think carefully and give me a straight answer.'

Fanch was ready to make any concession which would prolong the truce and keep him on the right side of this formidable man. He could not wriggle out of things now, but what if he could hold off the homework indefinitely by presenting the schoolmaster with some especially attractive red-herring? He looked at him out of the corner of his eye. Monsieur Cogan was an explorer at heart. Everyone knew his enthusiasm for archaeology and the active part which he had played in several excavations.

'What little spare time I've got after I've done all the jobs on the farm,' Fanch sighed, 'is taken up at the moment by a very odd business which is even keeping me awake at night. And the funny thing about it, Monsieur Cogan, is that you almost stumbled on the mystery just now, when you were watching those two holiday-makers who'd got hold of me.'

The schoolmaster seemed surprised.

'What were they after?'

'They wanted to make sure I'd help them explore the backwaters of the River Noyalo.'

'What would they be looking for in those swamps?'

'I don't quite know,' Fanch admitted. 'Your guess is as good as mine. They had some vague story of a boat going aground up there two or three months ago. But that doesn't seem very likely even with the extra high tides we had then. I don't know who owned her – one thing's for sure, it wasn't them, otherwise they wouldn't make such a mystery about it. In any case they've lost track completely of the wreck. The sketch-map they had with her position landed them straight in the mud.'

'Oh,' was all that Monsieur Cogan said. 'So there was a map, was there?'

He was obviously taking the bait, so Fanch struck hard.

'I guessed at once that there must be something else besides a boat. I expect you think the same?'

Monsieur Cogan nodded.

'What do you think: will they find her, or won't they?'

'I don't know,' said Fanch. 'The question isn't really important, is it? You were quite right, you know. I'd do much better spending the time I waste on it, swotting up at home.'

'Oh, no, you wouldn't!' Monsieur Cogan protested. 'This makes all the difference.'

He swung a masterful leg over the side and settled himself in the stern of the *Petit-Emile,* while a grinning Fanch slipped the rudder home. He was nearly up to his waist to get the boat clear and swung himself aboard easily in his turn. The sail filled gently and carried them swiftly out

92

into the open gulf between the end of the Isle-d'Arz and the Ile-d'Hur.

Fanch bubbled with delight at having so cleverly trepanned the terror of Saint-Arzhel.

'Now, let's hear all about it,' said Monsieur Cogan, securing the sheet.

He had the tiller under his right arm, while his left hand stroked the fringe of black hair which made his face seem oddly long. His fears at rest, Fanch now realized that he had a fine ally and that he must hold nothing back.

'It all started ten or twelve days ago by the wharf at Le Logéo. Uncle Job had sent me over with a couple of crates of lettuce for the Hotel Mahé. The first time I set eyes on Pat and Fredo, those two toughs who were after me just now, was when I was on my way back. They had a pal with them called Benny Cosquer. He couldn't take his eyes off the *Petit-Emile II,* the boat I salvaged from the mud several weeks ago, and cut my Certificate Exam to do it.'

They both laughed.

'I don't know how on earth he recognized her, and he wouldn't tell me. At any rate, from then on I didn't have a minute's peace. The three of them had been exploring the backwaters on foot from the landward side, and it had just about finished them. So then they split up. Pat and Fredo went off to hire a motor-boat while Benny went up the straits to keep an eye on the mouth of the River Noyalo. The others were supposed to pick him up there at high water the following day, but Benny seized the chance of their going to set off on my track – he had the map, and of course he hadn't breathed a word about the *Petit-Emile.* Two days later Monsieur Le Glohec brought us this odd sort of lodger. He settled in like a retired pirate, with one eye on the horizon in case his pals turned up, and the other on me and my boat, in which he seemed very interested indeed. I laid the bait for him myself by asking him out for a sail on the twenty-eighth, the day of the very high tide. We managed to get right up-river to the Seven Marshes and I showed him the exact spot where I'd salvaged the boat. Of course there wasn't anything else there and he got really angry when he couldn't find the slightest sign of another wrecked boat. When we got back to Goulvan his two pals were waiting for him. They forced him aboard their boat and gave him a real going-over. When I picked him off the La Teigne rock last night, he was in a dreadful state. For the moment he's gone to ground in the outbuildings on Cow Island. But he's a real tough nut and I don't think the others got anything out of him. So that's why they set on me.'

Monsieur Cogan was very impressed.

'And what do you know about the business, anyway?'

'Precious little. The sunken yacht looks like a cover-story to put outsiders off the scent. What's more I don't think any of the three had ever been up the river before, not even Benny, who, to give him his due, seemed quite at home at the tiller. They just turned up on our doorstep one day with information they'd stolen from someone else, pretending to be ordinary holiday-makers and hoping to get hold of something really good.'

'That's just it,' muttered Monsieur Cogan. 'And you haven't the slightest idea what they're after?'

'No.' Fanch was quite sincere. 'The thing that strikes me as odd, though, is the way they move heaven and earth to haul a boat out of the mud which won't be worth a penny more when they've salvaged her. If it's a cabin-cruiser or a sloop, she'll be in a fearful state of decay inside.'

'Some things don't decay,' the schoolmaster said quietly. 'And sometimes their age makes them more precious than gold to those who love them.'

'Benny did say something about a treasure,' Fanch admitted hesitantly. 'Irreplaceable, he said it was, too. I

94

didn't believe him. I thought it was only a way of getting me on his side. But you don't take kids in with that sort of story nowadays. .... All that hidden treasure has been dug up long ago, hasn't it?'

The regretful tone in his voice made Blackbeard smile. 'You're wrong there, Fanch. The most ordinary little pebble can turn out to be a treasure for someone who knows what he's looking for. The soil of Brittany is thick with it. I know what I'm talking about. Why don't you do some excavating on Goulvan one day, just where that little meadow sticks out to the west. I'll bet it won't be an hour before your pickaxe hits a dolmen, twenty-five thousand years old. These islands were once the tops of hills and nearly all of them have one or two megaliths on them.'

Fanch nodded, genuinely enthralled. His companion was well and truly involved and he had every hope of making him a friend, at the cost of the odd hour or two of study, snatched when the state of the tide stopped him sailing.

The *Petit-Emile* brought them back to reality, as her hull thumped over the choppy sea. The tide had turned and the pale blue of the bay was streaked by the darker lines of the fickle currents.

'Let's not get too carried away,' Monsieur Cogan went on, bringing her into the wind. 'The first thing we've got to do is get to the bottom of this story about the yacht. Why don't we have a word with your prisoner on Cow Island?'

'No. You'd be wasting your time if you tried to get Benny to talk. He'd only go out of his way to confuse you. But I do know someone who could set us on the right track. I'd like to have a word with Monsieur Tanguy, the Harbour Master at Locmariaquer. The only trouble is I wouldn't dare ask him by myself. We're not on very good terms for some time because of the *Petit-Emile,* the other one that caused me all this trouble, that is.'

He told the schoolmaster about the alarming incident of the Sunday when he had been with Lise, and of the way in which he had got rid of the boat.

'Take the tiller, and we'll go over to see Old Hogshead right away,' Monsieur Cogan decided. 'I'm not scared of the old boy. If he does know anything, he won't refuse to pass it on to me.'

The flood tide was running so fast that the launch from Vannes to Port Navalo was almost proceeding sideways to correct her drift. It was far too strong for any yacht, so there was not a sail in sight. Monsieur Tanguy lowered his binoculars, only to raise them almost at once and focus on a speck of red that had flashed in the sun on the far side of the straits.

'They must be crazy, trying to sail across with the flood tide running,' he said to Monsieur Stephani. 'It hasn't been done in years.'

'A big boat?' the Customs man asked with interest.

'Not on your life! A couple of lunatics in a little dinghy ... Good heavens!' Monsieur Tanguy added suddenly. 'I wonder if it's that young wrecker from the Ile-Goulvan.'

Monsieur Stephani took the glasses from him and had a look.

'That's Fanch all right!' he said after a minute. 'But I bet you a round of drinks he never makes it ... he doesn't carry enough sail, and there's hardly a breath of wind anyway.'

Old Hogshead never refused a bet.

'Done!' he said. 'That lad knows how to handle a boat.'

Kerpenhir Point hid the best part of the performance, but the next time they saw the red sail, it was on their side of the straits, speeding towards the harbour.

'He's made it!' Monsieur Stephani exclaimed. 'And he nearly beat that boat full of trippers ... How does the little devil do it?'

'He uses every ripple and cross-current like an outboard motor. A puff of wind in his sail at the right moment, and away he goes. But I never thought I'd see him round here after what happened the other evening.'

They walked down the stairs from the Harbour Master's office and on to the quay to see Fanch come in. The quay was crowded with local housewives and holiday-makers watching a motor drifter discharging her catch. It was then that Monsieur Tanguy recognized Fanch's passenger and laughed until the tears streamed down his cheeks at the sight of the boy sitting alongside his most dreaded enemy.

'Hi! Which of you caught the other?' he called to Monsieur Cogan. 'I'm surprised the lad didn't take the chance of having you over the side once he'd got you alone in the boat!'

Blackbeard came ashore laughing, while Fanch moored by the steps. The pot-bellied captain leaned forward to examine the boat and once more expressed some astonishment.

'Well, I'm glad to see the *Petit-Emile*'s back to her old size again,' he said sarcastically. 'That's not counting the mast and the sail . . . What's happened?'

'Oh,' said Fanch calmly, 'I took your advice. Some wrecks aren't worth salvaging, so I scuttled her at high tide. With a little luck she'd have come floating past Locmariaquer at about six o'clock last night, right past your doorstep as you might say.'

Monsieur Tanguy's face purpled with rage under his peaked cap.

'And I suppose you crossed the straits against the tide just to boast about your bit of sabotage? . . . You should have taken that wretched boat over to Langle and left it in Monsieur Riou's charge in his boatyard. Now you're coming straight up to my office with me. What you've done is barratry. There'll be a charge. I want your statement signed in front of two witnesses. The Customs Officer and the schoolmaster'll do very nicely.'

Fanch could think of no answer to this, but luckily the captain's lair was situated above the Café Poder. Before dealing with the wrecker, the men adjourned to the ground floor. There Monsieur Stephani at once settled his bet and Blackbeard politely bought a second round of drinks.

Monsieur Tanguy's assumed air of officiousness soon evaporated and Fanch, his mind at rest, sipped a cup of coffee as he listened to the three men gossiping. The fresh light of morning flooded into the room and the smoky ceiling shimmered gold with the reflection of the sea.

'Have you heard any talk of a yacht being lost or hidden somewhere in the gulf?'

Monsieur Cogan's abrupt question scarcely ruffled the Harbour Master.

'For the last month I've had half a dozen mysterious-looking visitors in my office every day after news of her. And every day they go out cursing my incompetence. There've been the police from Rennes and Paris, the top brass from the Coast Guard, insurance inspectors, newspaper men and all sorts of experts. The whole lot of them have had this one thing in their minds and they've bullied me with questions as though they expected me to produce a three-master from my filing cabinet . . . Goodness knows, they've been on at me about this wretched boat, day in day out, until I'm sick of the subject!'

Monsieur Stephani shook his head.

'And that's not the end of it, either. As soon as they've finished with poor old Tanguy, the whole gang come straight across the quay to the Customs Office and give me a dose of the same medicine. And all for the sake of some wretched boat that nobody's ever seen and which is

probably lying a hundred fathoms down off the cliffs of Belle-Ile!'

The Harbour Master looked round to make sure that they were not overheard. Then he leaned confidentially towards Blackbeard.

'Does the name *Berenice* ring a bell with you?'

Monsieur Cogan frowned and shook his head.

'I don't think so . . .'

Fanch had edged up to hear better.

'She's a red and white twelve-ton cabin cruiser, stolen at Easter with a full supply of fuel. She belongs to a wealthy industrialist from the North. The owner alerted the Coast Guard and they put out a Channel search. But the weather was appalling, and what with the mist and the rain-squalls, they drew a blank. All the same, one or two stations did pick up the *Berenice* and followed her passage towards the Atlantic. But every time, their messages arrived too late, the weather turned worse and the boat had changed colour, which made identification even more difficult. To cut a long story short, the last sighting was at dawn on 25 March off Kervilaouen – that is, to the west of Belle-Ile. After that she simply disappeared. Everyone round here thinks she must have gone down with all hands on the reefs of La Teignouse or Le Beniguet. But the office-wallahs who are looking so hard for her have another theory. According to them, there was enough fuel in the *Berenice*'s twin tanks to take her at least another hundred miles and lie up in some hiding-place along the coast . . .'

He tapped Monsieur Cogan on the shoulder and pointed to the stretch of sea sparkling beyond the window.

'And this is where she's supposed to be lying up – through the straits of Port Navalo. Since there's been no sign of her beyond this point, they think it's because she slipped into this inner sea and is hidden somewhere.'

'Who stole her?' asked Monsieur Cogan.

'The paid-hand of the *Berenice,* a fellow called Bena-fente (who, incidentally, has vanished), and probably a couple of accomplices ... I know what you're going to ask me, Cogan: what would they get out of such an escapade? They could never hope to dispose of the boat on this coast, after all. And what is so odd is the colossal fuss that is being made about the disappearance of an ordinary pleasure craft, when the loss must have been pretty well covered by insurance anyway. I can only suppose that the theft of the *Berenice* involved some other crime.

'But what?' asked Blackbeard. 'Your visitors must have told you.'

Monsieur Tanguy laughed.

'Never a word! I'd only to mention the possibility and they'd shut up like clams. It's the best way I've found so far of getting rid of them.'

'At the time,' Monsieur Stephani added, 'the news-papers were full of all sorts of crazy ideas – kidnapping, espionage, smuggling. But the *Berenice* hardly left French territorial waters once during her voyage. So she can't possibly have been used for a big smuggling operation.'

As he lifted his glass of Muscadet towards his purple nose, Old Hogshead stared at Fanch. The latter turned away in some confusion.

'In the first place,' the Harbour Master concluded, 'these gentlemen advised me to keep a close eye on any amateur salvage men. I only know of a dozen or so in my area and it didn't take me long to go round their yards. All the same, I wonder if it wouldn't be a good thing to send a dredger over to Goulvan to sift the sand there, one of these days ... What do you think, Fanch? And if you should ever run across a bit of the *Berenice,* no matter what size, you get a line on it and tow it straight over here as fast as you can.'

The full-throated laughter of the Customs man and the schoolmaster lightened the threat in the Harbour Master's words. But Monsieur Cogan wanted their future expeditions to be open and above board.

'Your investigators aren't the only ones after the wreck. They realize this, I suppose?'

Monsieur Tanguy winked.

'Of course they do. Can't you guess what their game is? If they give the suspects enough rope they'll show the way to the real culprits and perhaps – though I very much doubt it myself – to the *Berenice* herself – or what's left of her.'

Blackbeard thanked them, said good-bye to Old Hogshead and left the Café Poder with his sailor. They both felt as if they were walking a tight-rope.

'What this means,' Blackbeard told Fanch when they were outside, 'is that it's anybody's race. So long as the police don't stick their noses officially into the business, we can go right ahead.'

They conferred for a moment on the quayside while below them the buyers haggled over crates of still-wriggling sardines and mackerel.

'Don't trust Old Hogshead,' Fanch whispered. 'From the moment we left the café I've felt four or five pairs of eyes boring into the back of my neck. Take my word, they'll follow us with their binoculars until we're through the Straits of Pember, a good two miles away.'

'That's how I interpreted Monsieur Tanguy's last remark. There are hundreds of tourists sailing each day between Locmariaquer and Port Navalo. The Harbour Master keeps an eye on private craft, and Monsieur Stephani looks after the ferry and the launches from Vannes. I've a pretty shrewd idea that there are others in the background watching for anything odd or suspicious. Then they'll be on the telephone to someone at the other end of the gulf . . . How can we dodge them?'

'We know nothing,' said Fanch, an expression of complete innocence on his face. 'And we've got to make them go on thinking so. I've one or two things to buy in the village. Take the boat and let the tide carry you to the beach at Kerivau. Throw a spinner out over the stern; that might fool them. I'll meet you there.'

'And then?'

'Full sail for Cow Island. Benny's waiting for me. I'll be bringing him some new clothes so he can get properly dressed and we'll see what we can get out of him by kindness.'

'Do we really have to?'

Blackbeard was eager to take part in the adventure, but he wanted to keep his hands clean of anything unpleasant. Fanch was too innocent to share his scruples.

'Benny isn't too bad a chap,' he said with a laugh. 'And he's the only one who can take us to the *Berenice* and get us there first.'

6

Robbery on the Island

EVERY fifteen minutes Lise would come out of the yellow house, slip through the tamarisk hedge and run down to the lone pine. The rising waters began to catch its reflection and in the distance there was a flowering of sails on the horizon. At last, between the hump-backs of Hur and Huric she saw the *Petit-Emile* gliding gradually closer, now slim as a wing as the boat bore away, now broad and square as she came head on. When they were close enough to see her, Lise took off her head-scarf and waved it in the air.

Fanch never passed the Ile-Hervé without casting a glance at the solitary tree which stood up so gracefully against the skyline. He saw the signal at once and headed for the point. Lise waded into the water up to her knees to hold the boat off from grounding too hard.

'Did you know Benny was hiding in the buildings on Cow Island?'

'I fixed him up there last night,' Fanch answered, surprised. 'I felt so sorry for him. The others had half killed him and abandoned him on La Teigne. ... But what's happened?'

'Pat and Fredo came back on the dot of eleven, when the tide had covered the shoals round the island. Someone must have tipped them off. They went straight to the cowshed and dragged Benny out. He was too weak even to put up a fight.'

Fanch was horrified.

'Which way did they go?'

'I lost their boat behind Bilhervé Point. I expect they've got their camp well hidden on one of the beaches of the Isle-d'Arz.'

'We'll never catch them now,' Fanch sighed. 'All afternoon it'll be high water in the gulf. With her shallow draught and that outboard of hers, the *Waikiki* can always give us the slip even in a foot of water.'

His bitterness surprised Monsieur Cogan.

'Why are you worried? Remember the last thing Monsieur Tanguy said! Give the suspects plenty of rope and they'll lead us to the *Berenice*. And we're very nicely placed to keep an eye on them.'

Fanch shook his head obstinately.

'The whole thing falls down without Benny,' he said. 'He's the only one who can lead us right to the wreck.'

'No, he isn't,' Lise exclaimed. 'We've still got the map. What did you do with it?'

Fanch had completely forgotten about it in all the excitements of that morning. In any case, with his intimate knowledge of every inch of the gulf, the scrap of paper seemed to be something only necessary in an emergency.

'I left it at home on Goulvan. It's somewhere in the kitchen; though if Uncle Job's come across it he'll probably have used it for lighting his pipe.'

Up to now he had said little about the map to the schoolmaster; it wasn't that he was trying to play a double game, but simply because he had not thought it of any possible use in determining the course of the *Berenice*'s last voyage. Not even Benny himself had been able to make much of it, and had, in fact, gone hopelessly astray when trying to follow it. This is what Fanch now somewhat sulkily told his new companion, for Monsieur Cogan's face had lit up at the mention of it.

'You couldn't read it, that's all,' said the schoolmaster. 'Where is it? We must hurry and look at it again. Benny may well suspect that you removed it before you scuttled the boat. If he manages to persuade the others that you did, we'll soon see them back in full force in Sow Bay.'

The threat of danger roused Fanch, for not only did it add new excitement to the adventure, but it also drew the three of them closer together.

'Why don't you stay at the farm for a few days?' he suggested. 'The school's shut for the next couple of months, so there's nothing for you to do at Saint-Arzhel . . . Mamm would love to have you and she'd feel much safer with you around. And you'd be right on the spot to help me solve the riddle of the *Berenice*.'

Blackbeard swallowed the bait.

'I wouldn't want to cause any extra work,' he said, with a formal show of reluctance. 'Let's ask Mamm first.'

But a smiling Lise had not let go of the boat. She pointed to her bundle of clothes lying neatly on the beach in the shade of the pine-tree.

'You'll have to take me,' she said. 'Mama and Papa are letting me have a fortnight's holiday on Goulvan. It's all been arranged with the Guidics.'

Fanch helped his passenger aboard and then shoved the boat off with his oar. The sail filled and the *Petit-Emile* glided past the black posts which marked the oyster-parks. They shouted good-bye to the Jégos and their workmen, who were standing in front of the yellow house to watch them on their way. At first the Jégos stood in awe-struck amazement when they saw Monsieur Cogan crouched in the bows. Then the wind bore their hoots of laughter across the water and sped the *Petit-Emile* gaily on her journey to the leafy Ile-Goulvan.

Wondering at the honour done to her, Mamm Guidic herself showed the schoolmaster from Saint-Arzhel into the guest-room.

'The rogue who had it before you isn't past praying for. If he'd been able to stay a little longer, the loneliness and the fresh air would have cleared away the worst of his worries. And when you've been here a few days, you'll understand why Fanch only goes to school one day in three; don't think too badly of his laziness and his self-centredness, underneath it he's a very loyal person.'

Mamm was too sure of her power to beg favours, she only sought the opportunity of showing her kindness. Uncle Job stood in the doorway with the same welcoming smile on his face, while in the background Fanch and Lise screwed up their eyes like cats against the mid-day sun which blazed down on the yard and the fig-trees. Lunch was gay and carefree.

'I'm going over to Saint-Arzhel in a minute or two with twenty sacks of potatoes,' Uncle Job said when they were drinking coffee. 'Give me a note for your housekeeper, and I'll bring back whatever you need.'

Luckily he had not lit his pipe with the map from the *Berenice,* so that Fanch found the scrap of paper where he had left it.

'I'm no brighter than you,' Monsieur Cogan told the two children. 'Let's pool our local knowledge and maybe between us we'll be able to solve this riddle.'

Outside, the outboard motor of the big punt woke the echoes of Sow Bay. Mamm Guidic had disappeared with her shears and her basket in the direction of the garden. Blackbeard sat down at the long table with Fanch on his right and Lise on his left and all three wrestled with the secret of the stolen yacht.

The map was creased and grubby and spotted with oily finger-marks. The first thing which Monsieur Cogan noticed was that it had been torn from the edge of a nautical chart, for in places there were traces of a scale of latitude in miles. It had been very roughly drawn, doubtless with a ball-point pen, for it was scarcely affected by water stains, and showed, not the two sides of a river estuary, but one continuous line of coast with here and there dotted lines to show that the shore had not been properly charted.

At first sight, the chief care of the map-maker appeared to have been the choice of landmarks. The line of these little red points followed a winding course, each with an identifying note scrawled beside it. But the writing was so poor and the words so abbreviated as to be unreadable. At last, the true or supposed course of the *Berenice* curved away to the right into a wider, horn-shaped bay. There the intersection of two arrows showed where she had come to rest. The same hand had noted a bearing for each arrow. The writing was clearer and read:

S.E. Grey church tower beyond cross-shaped tree.
N.E. Red and white pylon slightly to right of parrot's
    beak.

The ghost-ship, stolen from Trouville harbour, lay where these two imaginary lines crossed.

'It's all Greek to me,' admitted a disappointed Fanch. 'Why, you can see a hundred grey church towers if you stand on Sow Rock and look round. And if the tree was cross-shaped at the end of March, you can be pretty sure that the summer's turned it into a round blob of green: we can forget about that!'

'The "parrot's beak" must be a rock,' said Monsieur Cogan, 'and whatever size the red and white pylon is, it must belong to an electricity grid-line. You can see pretty far inland from quite a few places along the coast, but you won't often find a landmark like that, so that one is some use ... But are you sure that this really is a map of the Noyalo Estuary? Let's suppose that Benny and his pals had never been in this part of the world before. In that case

they could have gone completely wrong from the start.'
Once more Fanch pored over the map and studied it for
some time before replying.

'No, this really is the right bank of the estuary. At the
bottom you can see the pier at Le Passage quite clearly,
and then the pocket formed by Le Hézo Bay, then the little
island forming a strait with Ar-Gouaren Point. The man
who drew the map didn't see the oyster-parks farther
up stream just below Noyalo and he didn't notice the big
bridge across the mouth of the Kernicol Lake either. And
yet, even if you were on the far side of the river, you
couldn't help seeing them, so it must either have been in
the dark or in very poor visibility. As a result he just drew
this bit as a dotted line until he could pick up his next
landmark. This is what proves that the map is genuine
and that the *Berenice* really did come up the estuary early
in the spring.'

This complete assurance impressed Monsieur Cogan,
who watched Fanch's finger move slowly upstream until
it stopped at the sixth of the red dots.

'The only letter you can see in all that scribble is the
"K" at the beginning. What do you make of it?'

The more he concentrated, the clearer Fanch found his
mind working.

'You can only see that landmark five months of the
year. It's the ruined walls of the old brick-works at Kerguenan. By the end of May they're completely hidden by
the trees and under-woods growing along the riverside.
Now, the morning we sailed up there, Benny, who kept
checking with this map the whole time, got the shock of
his life when there was nothing, where he expected to see
a massive building. I didn't take any notice at the time, but
now we've got the map in front of us, his knowing about
it makes me wonder.'

'It looks as if Benny is the guilty party,' Blackbeard declared. 'Even if he wasn't at the wheel himself on the *Berenice*'s last voyage, someone who was on board went over the course with him point by point with the help of this map . . . But let's go on.'

Fanch and Lise were almost lying on the table on either side of the schoolmaster in their endeavour to study the map.

'The next four landmarks lead us right into the dark again,' Fanch went on. 'Number 10 lies well inland, and so it could be an isolated farmhouse on the ridge by Rose-en-Sincé. After that we're in the Seven Marshes. Benny thought he knew where he was for a moment, and then he realized he didn't and our partnership nearly broke up in a fight. All the same, Monsieur Cogan, I promise you that I really did salvage the boat from the marshes. When I heaved her out of the mud her white hull was hardly damaged, and she was the *Petit-Emile II,* the one that made so much trouble for me . . . You heard how Old Hogshead carried on this morning? I still got the blame whether I kept her or got rid of her. I suppose what I should have done was put her on a trolley, hitched up a couple of cart-horses and wheeled her into the Harbour Master's office with the mud dripping off her.'

They laughed and then pored over the map again in silence.

'That's where the *Berenice* finished up,' Fanch said after a moment, 'in that broad inlet shaped like a goat's horn. I've never seen anything like it in the Seven Marshes. You can just make out the old dyke that fed the salt-pans under all those reeds. Beyond that it's all cracked red mud that the tide only covers about twice a year. You couldn't get a canoe across it at the highest water.'

'The helmsman of the *Berenice* could have gone quite wrong if he was steering by dead reckoning in poor visibility . . . What's upstream from the marshes?'

'On one side of the river you've got the oyster-parks at Saint-Goustan, and on the other are the saltings where they put sheep out to graze. Beyond that the river ceases to be tidal. It wouldn't matter what kind of yacht it was, if it ran aground in flat country like that, it would stand out like a cathedral.'

Blackbeard was still smiling, but then his expression turned grave.

'It's not very hard to realize that exceptional conditions helped the *Berenice* to disappear. At present we just don't seem able to imagine what they were.'

'The Little Sea doesn't often mislead me,' Fanch answered coldly. 'I know it better than most. My only master is the old man at Langle.'

'But Monsieur Riou is far too good a sailor to bother very much about backwaters like this,' the schoolmaster said cheerfully. 'A high spring tide, backed by a strong sou'-wester, often goes a good three feet above the usual high-water mark. We hardly notice it here on the cliffs and the harbour-walls, but in lonely uninhabited places the flood sometimes penetrates far inland. It only lasts an hour or two, and when the tide turns nobody knows it has ever happened ... Take my word for it, Fanch, the *Berenice* really did come to rest where those two arrows cross, one freezing foggy morning when you were tucked up snug in bed behind the thick walls of this farmhouse.'

Fanch's blood was up. He smoothed the strip of paper with the flat of his hand.

'Good, you may be right. Anyway, let's try to find this bay by going back over the bearings one by one and filling in from our own knowledge the stretches this idiot only dotted in.'

Armed with compass, pencil and ruler, they set to work, like a pair of prize pupils sharing the same desk, for Lise soon tired of the game. She went out into the yard for a minute or two and when she came in wandered slowly round the vast room, darkening with the dusk.

She had a sharper pair of eyes than Blackbeard and she was not so abstracted as Fanch. She still possessed that youthful satisfaction in the observation of familiar things.

'There's the Horn behind you!' she said suddenly.

Fanch and Blackbeard turned round, bewildered, to look at the old map hanging on the wall, the glass over it a sheet of gold in the evening light. Monsieur Cogan was the first to get up and make a closer inspection.

The old line of the upper reaches of the estuary roughly resembled a goat's head, with its snub nose at Saint-Goustan and its pair of horns butting inland. They were of unequal length and the lower one cut far in below the hills around Sincé. Monsieur Cogan checked the last voyage of the *Berenice* point by point against that yellow, one-hundred-and-fifty-year-old map – and everything fitted.

The helmsman of the *Berenice* had made no mistake when he made the Seven Marshes stretch so far. It was the fickle sea which had betrayed his accomplices, leaving the yacht high and dry where the two arrows crossed in a deserted, unhealthy mud-choked swamp, shunned by the islanders and as inaccessible as the undersea reefs of the open sea.

Fanch instinctively knew the rhythm of the tides and had no need of a timetable to guide his wanderings.

'It's too late now. The next high water's about midnight. We can't do anything until tomorrow.'

'Neither can the others,' said Blackbeard, 'so we've still a chance of getting there first. But remember, we don't want to miss the tide tomorrow afternoon.'

It was the middle of the night when Fanch woke. He was clearheaded and alert. At first he lay on his back in bed, staring at the stars beyond the lighter patch of window. Then he listened to the indistinct and mingled sounds from outside. Someone was walking very quietly in front of the house. The footsteps ceased for a second or two, and then their owner was off again, brushing against the walls.

Without making a sound, the boy got out of bed and leaned out of the window. In the yard, just below him, a man was standing, facing the gateway and smoking a cigarette. The glow lit up his face suddenly and Fanch was relieved to see that it was Blackbeard. He whistled softly to attract his attention and Monsieur Cogan looked up with a nervous start.

'Get dressed quickly and come down here,' he whispered. 'But mind you don't wake up Mamm and Lise.'

Slipping on singlet and trousers, Fanch went barefoot downstairs and across the kitchen. With immense care he opened the door.

'Uncle Job's gone over to the cliffs to take a look,' Monsieur Cogan explained. 'A motor-boat's been hanging round the island for the last ten minutes.'

'The hum of the engine must have woken me up,' said Fanch. 'You can hear better upstairs.'

They stopped talking to listen to the dull buzz that came over the clear night air, now deadened behind some headland, now sounding loud in the distance.

'Let's go along the seaward side of the heath,' Fanch suggested.

Blackbeard shook his head.

'We can't leave Mamm and Lise on their own. Someone must stay to look after the house.'

'You scared of something?'

'No, but Uncle Job's careful. He hasn't forgotten the way those two strangers burst into the house the other day.'

Fanch listened again. The noise was getting louder and seemed to come from the south of the island.

'It's an outboard-motor running at full throttle. It could be the *Waikiki* . . .'

They tiptoed round the house to stand outside the guest-room, where they had a good view of a wide segment of coastline. It was nearly high water and opposite them they could see the dim lights of Saint-Arzhel twinkling level with the black line of the sea. The night was warm, with only the suggestion of a landbreeze bearing the lightest scent of distant woods and meadows.

A little later, Uncle Job came silently back through the gateway, his shot-gun under his arm.

'It makes me very angry,' he muttered. 'I've a good pair of eyes and I distinctly saw the boat when it rounded Sow Point. It's the same one all right. There were three of them aboard, so it looks as if our friend Benny's made peace with his pals. Five minutes later, when I got to the end of the cliff, I saw her coming back. There's only one man in her now, I'm sure of that.'

'That means two of them have landed on Goulvan,' said Blackbeard. 'They may even have come ashore at different places, so as to take the farm in the rear. I don't like the sound of it.'

'As soon as the engine of that confounded boat stops,' Uncle Job went on, 'it'll mean that the third has come ashore on one of our beaches. We shan't be able to count a hundred before we have those thugs on our backs. I could still go down and guard Sow Bay, but that would only leave the two of you for the house.'

'It's too risky,' Monsieur Cogan agreed. 'We'd much better all stick together here in the yard.'

'Right!' said Uncle Job and turned to Fanch. 'You stand in the gateway. If you see anyone coming up the drive, give us a whistle. Then go straight back into the house and lock the door behind you. I'll keep in the shade of the fig-trees and cover the garden side. Monsieur Cogan, will you stay by your room and keep a good look-out over the fields? If they come that way, drop back and join me in the yard. A good charge of buck-shot'll soon have them running.'

They scattered to their posts. Silently Fanch crossed the yard and his slender shape was swallowed by the gloom of the gateway: Blackbeard was already round the corner of the house, while Uncle Job peered about him for a moment and then disappeared under cover of the fig-trees. Each waited at his post as the moon rode high in the heavens, its cold beams frosting the long house front with its barred shutters. Upstairs nobody stirred.

Minutes passed. The sound of the outboard had grown closer. It seemed to hug the northern end of the island. Then suddenly it cut out and the watchers felt the darkness at once full of danger. Fanch stared along the road. The overhanging trees formed an impenetrable arch, but at the end of the tunnel Sow Bay glittered in the moon-light. This was the route the *Waikiki* took. She had enough way to come gliding in over the silvery sea, and ground, like some big black fish, on the beach. The burly figure of either Pat or Fredo clambered over the side and came hesitantly up towards the farm.

Fanch was so angry that he completely forgot Uncle Job's instructions. Instead of warning the others, he left his shelter and came slinking down from tree to tree to meet the intruder. It was Pat. Fanch recognized him from some way off by his fatness and the way his shoulders rolled as he walked. A short sharp whistle came from the direction of the yard. At once Pat started to run. Twenty yards from the gateway Fanch stuck out his foot and as Pat came crashing to the ground, leapt on his back like a panther.

'Let me go!' Pat yelled. 'Get off, you swine!'

He rolled about wildly in an effort to throw off his attacker. Fanch held firm, exchanging blow for blow.

Up at the farm things were not going well. Blackbeard mistook the whistle for Fanch's warning, came out of cover too soon and was laid out cold by a violent blow on the back of the head. At the same moment Uncle Job was taken abruptly in the rear and let off his shot-gun into the fig-trees, waking every animal in the outbuildings and all the birds for miles around. They fled with startled squawks into the moonlight.

Fanch was still struggling with the burly Pat. He heard someone running through the gateway and craned his neck to see who it was. At first he thought it was Monsieur Cogan, but it turned out to be Benny and Fanch had to let go, ducking aside to avoid a swinging fist.

'You change sides pretty fast,' he said scornfully to Benny. 'Wasn't the shed on Cow Island comfortable enough for you?'

Pat got up, panting for breath, his eyes squinting as he looked round for his opponent. Fanch scowled at the two men from the shadows.

'You won't catch me. I can run ten times round the island without losing my breath.'

'Shut up, you little fool!' Benny broke in angrily. 'You come back to the farm with us right away. If you're thinking of making a bolt for it, just remember that the others'll suffer if you do.'

Fanch had to give in to this threat and came unwillingly out of the undergrowth.

'After you,' he said, pointing to the gateway. 'I'm not going into my own house with a pair of crooks on my heels.'

'Want a thick ear!' Pat bellowed.

Fanch laughed.

'You should have given me one just now when we were

cheek to cheek . . . In you go. I'm right behind you.'

And so they came into the yard, the two men leading and occasionally glancing over their shoulders to make sure that the boy had not given them the slip. Uncle Job and Blackbeard were sitting on the stone seat in front of the house, held at pistol-point by Fredo. The defenders of Goulvan were a sorry sight. Shame and anger at having been caught by surprise showed on Uncle Job's face, while Monsieur Cogan dabbed at the blood from the cut on his head.

At first Benny tried to break the door down, but it was too strong for his shoulder.

'Which of you three has the key?'

Fanch took it out of his pocket and threw it disdainfully on to the ground.

'Take it,' he said slowly. 'There's no money and nothing worth your while smashing the furniture for. But I warn you, if any one of you sets foot on the staircase, he'd better look out.'

'We're not going to bother the old crow,' Fredo sneered. 'She can sleep in peace.'

Benny knew his way about, so he went in first and lit the lamp. Fredo then forced his prisoners to their feet and hustled them through the doorway. Fanch had not stirred.

'You first,' he said coldly to Pat. 'And keep away from me or we may find ourselves fighting again. Even if you beat me this time, I'll still be able to do quite a bit of damage to you.'

The thug did not dare to argue, and Fanch came in last, leaving the door open behind him on the moonlit yard. The light indoors made some of the men's faces look cruelly ugly. The swelling had gone down on Benny's, after the beating-up he had had the night before, but his scratches and his black eye gave him a sinister look. Pat and Fredo were red-faced and sweating and their ferrety little eyes darted round, bright with greed. Fanch made a wide detour to take his place behind the table with Uncle Job and Monsieur Cogan and glare ferociously at the intruders.

'I'm taking a good look at you,' said the schoolmaster, 'to make sure I know you when I see you again. And that'll be sooner than you think.'

As he brushed against the table, Fanch picked something up. Now he held it up firmly in his hand.

'I know what you're after,' he said to Benny. 'Don't bother to turn the house upside-down ... here's your map. Take it and get out!'

Benny laughed.

'To be quite honest, Fanch, we aren't interested in that one. I may be a bit slow to start with, but in the end I always get what I want. My stay on Goulvan may have been short and sweet, but it's brought me something useful.'

The others were already in the secret. Pat went straight to the far end of the room and unhooked the map from the wall. The frame slipped and fell with a crash of glass to the floor. The yellowed paper of the map fluttered free of the wreckage, and in a flash Benny had torn off the part which interested him and pushed it under his singlet.

'Thanks and good-bye!'

Together the three backed away towards the door, grinning triumphantly at the islanders. But their gaiety did not last long. There was suddenly a tremendous clatter and down the staircase came a black-clad figure brandishing a six-foot broom. Madame Guidic had dressed in far too much of a hurry to fasten her cap properly and it wobbled comically from side to side. Either she did not, or pretended not to see the pistol Fredo pointed.

119

'Where's Lise?' she screeched. 'Where is she, you wretches?'

And then she started to swing her broom. The first stroke caught Benny on his battered face and sent him tumbling through the doorway. Bowing to the storm, Pat and Fredo scrambled over their accomplice and then hauled him clear like a sack of coal. The trio then took to their heels.

As soon as Mamm and the others came out, their fears vanished, for there was Lise standing like a slender white statue in the middle of the yard.

'Here I am,' she gasped. 'Don't get upset. Uncle's shot woke me up. I sneaked through the larder window to see what was going on.'

She was laughing with relief. From the beach came the sound of the *Waikiki*'s engine starting up. Sadly and wearily Uncle Job was the first to take the blame. 'Age is a sad thing for an old soldier who fought on the Hauts-de-Meuse and at Vauquois. Why, I can't even shoot straight now.'

'There's nothing to be sorry about,' said Fanch. 'You didn't kill anyone. In any case, it wasn't worth bothering about.'

Blackbeard looked white. Mamm thought he was badly hurt and tried to take him indoors.

'No!' he said angrily. 'All I got out of the whole silly business is a lump on the back of the head ... And it's all my own careless fault, what's more. Your night air's a bit too strong for someone who spends half his time cooped up indoors.'

Fanch attempted to console him.

'Half the time I was hitting that fat thug I was doing it for you. Every other one I gave him, I said "Here, take that from me for Blackbeard!"'

'Where's your hand?' Monsieur Cogan said in cheerful

resignation. 'We'll find a way of getting round this school business.'

Lise was still laughing and crumpling a paper bag in her hands.

'I've played them the dirtiest trick ever ...' she said in a low voice. 'Papa talked about it the other day, when we were wondering what to do about someone who hangs round our oyster-parks to steal the tiles ... But I still don't know whether it's going to work. You see, while you were all so busy in the yard, I ran down to the beach and poured sugar into the *Waikiki*'s petrol-tank.'

'How much?' asked Uncle Job, hopefully.

'About two pounds, I should think. All that was in this bag anyway ... I hope Mamm won't mind me taking it.'

The two men and the boy roared with laughter.

'Well done!' said Blackbeard. 'Thanks to you our stock in the *Berenice* has gone rocketing up ... Just listen for a minute, Lise.'

The group round her stopped talking. The muted hum of the *Waikiki* swung along under the cliffs and died away to the south of the island. Every now and then the regular beat of the engine was broken by a backfire and then, a little later, it coughed once and died away altogether.

'The currents will carry them all over the place,' Uncle Job remarked with immense satisfaction. 'Considering things at their brightest from their point of view, they'll have to wait for daylight to strip and clean the engine, or else hire another boat.'

'And we'll be well ahead of them again,' Blackbeard added. 'We'll be the only ones to go up on the next high tide to the Seven Marshes. The fools didn't even realize that the map was useless now. It was Fanch they should have taken ...'

7

Grey Church Tower beyond Cross-Shaped Tree

LISE was kneeling in the bows, leaning right out like a figurehead, her hair ruffled by the breeze. Blackbeard sat amidships, snoozing in the shadow cast by the sail. He had tied a red bandana over his head to hide the dressing on his cut, and it made him look still more like a pirate.

'All you need is a gold ring in your left ear!' Fanch chuckled.

Monsieur Cogan opened one eye and the lines in his face softened into a smile,

'Think you can find your way? It's been no good my looking. From sea-level, the coast seems as flat as a desert.'

'Don't you worry,' Fanch said. 'We've got the wind and the tide behind us and in another half-hour you'll see the jetty and the red buoy of Le Passage dead ahead. Once we're through the straits all we've got to do is hug the bank and let the tide do the rest. The wind's swung round since this morning and it's bringing up a few clouds. We'll have a good strong tide under us and it'll take us right into the Seven Marshes.'

'Will it be as high as it was on your last trip?'

'I'm afraid not. But I know all the paths through the swamp and we'll not need to get our feet wet while we look for these famous bearings marked on Benny's map.'

'Pat must have snaffled it off the table before they left,' Blackbeard complained. 'Can you remember the leading marks scrawled at the point of the arrows?'

' "South-East: Grey church tower beyond cross-shaped tree.

' "North-East: Red and white pylon beyond parrot's beak",' Fanch recited. 'I shan't forget them in a hurry. All the boats in the bay have the same sorts of mark to find the best fishing grounds and to keep themselves on course. When I was eight and had a little seven-foot dinghy I used the same sort of bearings to catch the currents from one island to another, though then I didn't know that's what I was doing . . . Look over Lise's head. The current carrying us now runs along the line of Le Hézo church tower and the black chimney of the chemical factory way beyond it. You can pick out both of them quite clearly from here. It's easy. But if I lay off to starboard, the boat will get out of the invisible river and we'll go drifting off to the oyster-parks at Moustérian.'

'All right, all right!' Blackbeard seemed quite convinced. 'I take my hat off to you. But keep your eyes open and the boat on course, and you can show us what you mean another day.'

They had left Goulvan just as the tide was beginning to turn. Mamm Guidic herself had followed them down to Sow Bay with a heavy basket stuffed with provisions for three hearty appetites. Uncle Job had just come back from Cow Island with his shot-gun slung over his left shoulder.

'Don't you laugh at me. One day I'll succeed in getting a shot at that scum. Meanwhile I'm not leaving Mamm alone on the farm. I'll wait till you get back before I pop over to Saint-Arzhel.'

Neither of the old folk believed the story of the *Berenice*. As they saw it, it was just a cover for some commonplace crime. The deserted islands and the deep inlets of the Little Sea provided admirable concealment for smugglers or dealers in stolen goods, who could easily outwit

123

the Customs men. But when Mamm and Uncle Job based this theory on a hundred or more similar stories which had passed into local history, they were wrong.

Monsieur Cogan, on the other hand, had been struck by the odd way in which the marauders had gone about things. Their clumsiness suggested that they had no skill or experience of smuggling, but the prospect of making a large profit very quickly showed itself in their wild behaviour, their ceaseless quarrels and the lack of planning which sent them running off in all directions when cleverer men would have bided their time.

And what really lay at the end of the quest? It might well be an object to which distance lent glamour and which had drawn treasure-hunters and criminals from afar. Blackbeard himself had haunted museums, sale-rooms and the back rooms of antique-shops, and knew what value could be placed on something very old, or very rare.

Lise and Fanch listened to what he said with polite interest, but their thoughts were miles away.

'And what about you?' Monsieur Cogan asked Fanch. 'What are you looking for?'

'The only things I'm fond of are boats,' Fanch answered, without hesitation. 'I'm waiting for the moment when we find the hull of the *Berenice* lying in the mud, and I climb down into the cockpit to open the cabin door. It doesn't much matter what we find behind it, I want to be there, that's all.'

The girl in the bows had not said a word, and Blackbeard now turned to her.

'And what about you?'

'I'm not looking for anything,' she said with a shy smile. 'All I want to do is share something nice with Fanch.'

The mainland was closer now, and soon the white pier

of Le Passage emerged from the blue water. The current was not very strong, but there was a steady wind from the north-west to drive them through the narrows. Over towards Montsarac, about a dozen cars were parked along the road leading to the headland. At the end of the wharf, the ferry was taking on passengers. Opposite them, holiday-makers strolled along the quayside and stared at the yachts which were beginning to dot the northern waters of the gulf.

Fanch and Blackbeard looked round when a flash told them they were being watched through binoculars, but they were relieved of this scrutiny once they passed the shoals off Le Hézo. At last the estuary lay before them, calm as a lake, with only the shadow of an occasional passing cloud to darken the water and the fields which bordered it.

A little farther on they came up with a yellow canoe. Two-thirds of it was filled with the baggage belonging to its crew, a pair of unwashed, unshaven campers, who shouted a cheerful greeting across the water.

'We're going up to Poteau Rouge,' called one of them. 'Do you know it?'

'It's a fine camping-site,' Fanch answered. 'But don't stop too long for lunch on the way. The tide'll be against you after four this afternoon.'

Some time later they heard the whine of an outboard-motor coming up fast astern. Fanch at once laid an oar within handy reach along the thwarts. He was looking forward to repelling boarders, being more than ever determined to hit hard. The outboard came up fast with a roar, but it was not the *Waikiki*. (The latter had doubtless been lying since daybreak on some lonely beach on the Isle-aux-Moines, completely immobilized by the sticky mixture in her tank.) The newcomer was painted bright red. At the wheel was a man wearing a yachting cap. He passed the *Petit-Emile* and when he was some way ahead turned back, slowed down to stare suspiciously at the vessel and her crew, and then made off for the straits as fast as he had come.

'Well, his business is pretty plain,' Blackbeard laughed. 'He's made the round-trip especially to take a look at us, and it's obvious we don't interest him.'

Five minutes later, when the *Petit-Emile* was sailing past the first oyster-parks in the estuary, the whine of the outboard sounded once more in the distance. The red-painted boat was coming up at top speed and heading straight for them.

'You're not to go any farther!' the man at the wheel bellowed, as soon as they were within hailing-distance. 'Change course at once; come back and tie up at Le Passage. We're waiting for you there.'

As the stranger reduced speed to come alongside, Fanch got the oar ready.

'What's the matter with you?' Blackbeard shouted back. 'We can sail here if we want to, and we can all swim . . . You just push off!'

The other screamed, 'I know who you are! You're one of the three crooks who wrecked my best boat on the Mare's Nose! They telephoned the news to me from Locmariaquer. Now I've got you, and I'll have your two pals before the day's out!'

Blackbeard snatched off the red bandana.

'You're off your head! I'm Noel Cogan, the schoolmaster from Saint-Arzhel. Everyone from Vannes to Sarzeau knows me. I'll come with you if you like, but I warn you that defending an action for slander will cost you as much as the boat you've lost.'

The man calmed down at once and came gently alongside, unconcerned by the oar which Fanch brandished.

126

'Have you proof of identity? Show me ... Then we'll see.'

Blackbeard did not protest. In a few moments all was settled.

'The whole business makes me wild,' sighed the unfortunate man who had hired out the *Waikiki*. 'From early this morning I've been round every harbour and island after those three crooks. Unless I can get my hands on them, the insurance will only cover half my loss, and the boat's holed like a colander and the engine's no more than scrap ... Sorry to have bothered you.'

The outboard snarled and he hurried away. Blackbeard was highly delighted.

'You really did it that time!' He laughed at Lise.

'It may not be her fault,' Fanch pleaded. 'Our visitors last night had plenty of time to ground the *Waikiki* on a sandbank, but they were in so much of a hurry that they must have jumped overboard and left her to drift away.'

They pulled into the shore above Noyalo, tying up under a willow tree whose branches dangled in the water. In its shelter they ate their lunch without leaving the boat. Fanch tucked in heartily, but that did not stop him keeping an eye on the estuary.

All they saw proceeding up- or down-stream were the oyster-growers' punts returning from their parks.

The comic entertainment came with their dessert. The bearded campers paddled slowly past, chewing enormous sandwiches. They never noticed the dinghy nestling among the branches. But they did not get very far. The boatman again came into sight, vanished up-river with a noise like thunder, and reappeared towing the canoe with the two indignant campers protesting wildly. On board the *Petit-Emile,* they laughed until they cried and then Blackbeard stood up.

'This is the second time you've picked the wrong

people!' he called to the boatman. 'Take a closer look at them. Your customers for the *Waikiki* were a much uglier bunch.'

'How do you know that?'

'They broke into our place last night,' Fanch answered.

'You can't see very much behind those beards,' argued the boatman, beside himself with rage. 'The only way I'll ever find those thieves of mine is by collaring every suspicious character I can lay hands on!'

'Then let that pair go at once,' Monsieur Cogan told him. 'Your three ruffians are nothing like these water-gipsies.'

The owner of the *Waikiki* reluctantly slipped the tow-rope, and went off on his search once more. One stroke of her paddles brought the yellow canoe alongside the *Petit-Emile*.

'My name's Manoel,' said the man in the bows. 'You can tell me from my brother, because my beard's bushier. His friends call him Picou . . . and that includes you. Thanks awfully for getting us out of that mess.'

'I shouldn't complain,' said Monsieur Cogan, compla-cently stroking his own beard. 'You're looking for adventure, aren't you? Well, there's one here all ready for you. As soon as we've shared out this apple-pie, we'll make a start.'

Mamm's apple-pie was every bit as good as Aunt Annick's. Manoel and Picou nearly swallowed their whiskers too. Fanch examined the yellow canoe carefully as he ate. If all the baggage were unloaded, the plywood hull would be light to carry on sturdy shoulders. When Fanch started to explain his plan, Monsieur Cogan did not inter-rupt.

'Don't you worry about getting to your camping-site,' Fanch began. 'Poteau Rouge isn't far away, and the *Petit-Emile* will get you there in no time. We're going in that direction. You can save your energy and we'll give you a tow as far as the Seven Marshes. What's the name of your canoe?'

'She hasn't got a name,' Manoel said with some embarrassment. 'She's just a hired boat with a number – *Two*.'

'Here's to *Two*!' Fanch shouted. 'She'll take us to the *Berenice*.'

The north-west wind blew steadily and the *Petit-Emile* easily broke the barricade of reeds, making a breach through which the *Two* came bobbing like a duck in her wake. It was high tide, but, to his dismay, Fanch noticed that the water was a good eighteen inches lower than on his previous trip.

Nonetheless they had no difficulty in getting through the patches of rush and green water-weed which covered the surface of the channel. Strange birds fled, squawking and shrilling, from their hiding places. Cloud-shadows chased overhead, darkening the ill-defined edges of the water.

Fanch had a hard job poling the boat through the second barrier with the oar. The reeds were already dead and parted with a dry rustle to close lazily behind the two craft. At last they were in clear water with a firm bottom and they emerged into a lake surrounded by dry land. The *Petit-Emile* was steered over to a tamarisk-fringed bank. Nearby was the gloomy inlet where Fanch had found the white boat.

'This is as far as my old boat will go,' he told Monsieur Cogan. 'But the *Two* would float in a puddle, and you can carry on the search with her.'

'I've memorized the bearings,' Blackbeard assured him.

'Right, then you carry on with the campers and keep going along the channel. When you come to a dyke you can easily pick her up and carry her over. Lise and I will go on foot through the bushes.'

Manoel and Picou put all their gear in the *Petit-Emile*, and Monsieur Cogan got into the canoe between them. Away went the three bearded gentlemen, sitting in line.

'We've come best out of this,' said Fanch, taking Lise by the hand. 'I've known that old map at home ever since I was a little boy. It may not have a gold mark in the place where the *Berenice* went down, but I'm sure that we'll find it in half the time on foot. The grey church tower on Benny's map must be the one at Kérandré. If we keep to the tamarisks we'll soon be able to spot it. Over on the far bank, Blackbeard will see the red and white pylon and the "parrot's beak" before we do, they're further to the north. Once that happens, we'll be very close to the lost boat. We'll simply have to keep our eyes open.'

A very low dyke covered with mares' tails closed the end of the lake. The yellow canoe reached it first, found a breach in it and vanished with a few strokes of the paddles. Fanch and Lise had to push their way through the undergrowth to this frontier. They cut away to the right to reach the bank and suddenly they were in another world. The red chequer-board of the old salt-pans stretched away in a broad curve bordered by thickets of osiers and dwarf-aspens.

'The goat's horn must start from here,' Fanch muttered. 'We shan't see anything for a minute or two. So keep going and follow me.'

Away in the distance the crew of the canoe were making their first portage, slowly crossing from one pool to the next, carrying their craft above their heads. Fanch and Lise ventured cautiously along the overgrown path bordering the salt-marsh. At last they reached the square salt-pans and were greeted by a chorus of quacks from the water fowl. Most of the area was given over to rushes and pools of stagnant water which in places seemed to be no more than a foot deep.

'It's impossible!' Fanch groaned. 'A large boat could never have come as far as this ... Look, even the canoe's had to give up.'

Blackbeard and his companions had emerged from the thick green undergrowth, leaving their vessel on a little mound. They continued along the low banks which rose only a few inches above the surface and separated the salt-pans from one another. The group gradually moved away, Monsieur Cogan leading. When he waved his arms it was plain that he had discovered something.

'And I bet it isn't the boat,' said Lise, 'or we should have seen her too.'

'No,' said Fanch, 'he must have spotted one of his marks. Either the red and white pylon or the rock shaped like a parrot's beak ... Let's keep going.'

On they went along the path beside the salt-pans. It ran dead straight and soon brought them level with the others moving forward on the far bank, small figures half-a-mile away almost lost against the green background of undergrowth. Fanch suddenly stopped.

'I can see the grey church tower,' he said and raised his arm. 'It's just sticking up above that clump of green over there. That must be the wood near Trévinel ... Now where's that wretched tree?'

They set off again, more slowly this time, their eyes firmly fixed on the church tower which gradually emerged from behind the wood. Then Lise gave a stifled cry.

'There it is, Fanch!'

The cross-shaped tree was not covered by a mass of leaves. It stood all by itself on a mound where the far bank fell right away. It was dead; the wind and rain had stripped the bark away and left it standing stark and white like a cross against the bright sky.

They went on, their eyes glued to the far bank. Fifty yards, and Fanch saw the marks come into line, the grey church tower rising exactly above the cross-shaped tree.

'The *Berenice* must be over there, at the point where Blackbeard's path and ours cross ... Let's hurry. But watch how you go; don't step into a mud hole.'

Still they could see nothing, not so much as the top of the cabin, and Fanch's hopes of discovering the boat in this morass were fading fast. Beyond them, Blackbeard was waving his arms to show that he, too, had picked up the bearings. The two groups began to move diagonally towards one another, stepping carefully along the narrow banks of earth which divided the salt-pans.

It was fifteen minutes before they met. Half-way there, Fanch looked to the north to see the distant red and white pylon and twisted fragment of rock which guided Monsieur Cogan. At last they met face to face and stared around them. Their spirits sank, for there was nothing, not the slightest scrap of ship's timber to be seen.

'We've been had!' the campers were saying. 'And we don't think it's very funny, either ... You were talking about a yacht just now ... well, there isn't enough water here to float a matchbox.'

Fanch's keen eyes scanned the distance to make sure they were on the right bearings. Suddenly he said to Blackbeard, 'I made a mistake this morning when I told you what was written on the map. From where we are, the rock's lined up on the pylon. But what the map really said was *"red and white pylon slightly to the right of the parrot's beak."* We ought to push on a bit farther along the line I've been following, and within a hundred yards or so we should find the exact spot marked on the map.'

In single file they set off along the bank which in places crumbled under their feet. The quackings stilled at their approach and the rushes stirred with secret scurryings.

Fanch led the way, watching the north-eastern marks open out correctly. In this fashion they skirted three salt-pans, only to be pulled up short by a far deeper cut, which must originally have been one of the canals feeding salt-water to the pans. A black wooden sluice-gate divided it from the reed-choked pan.

The *Berenice* lay behind this black screen. Her moss-covered hull had sunk so low into the mud that Fanch only noticed it at the very last moment as he was bending down to examine the rusty wheel which operated the

sluice. His triumphant shout brought the others running. All hope had vanished long before and the discovery left them speechless and at first almost scared.

The glory had departed from the smart cabin-cruiser stolen from Trouville Harbour. The chrome fittings, the varnish and the cabin lights were covered by a layer of red mud. The windshield by the wheel was shattered and the wireless mast hung over the port side, a pitiable, twisted wreck. In the well of the cockpit lay a puddle of oily, stagnant water. The cabin door was half-open to reveal the pools of dark, rubbish-strewn water within.

'When she was new, the *Berenice* must have cost her owner at least two hundred thousand francs,' Fanch said half to himself. 'That's real money! And now she isn't worth a thing. And it would take you six months to dredge a channel for her down to the river . . . What a mess she's in! It doesn't look as though we'll find much aboard her.'

'You go first!' said Blackbeard. 'Don't touch anything. Just make sure we can get aboard without breaking our necks.'

The boy scrambled down the side of the cut, holding on to the long grass. He felt for the stern with his foot, pressed gently at first and then let down his full weight. But the hull had settled so comfortably into the mud that it budged no more than if it had been a concrete pill-box. From there he jumped down on to the cockpit seats and surveyed the wreckage round the wheel.

Fanch went forward and pushed the cabin door right open. The change from bright sunlight to gloom prevented him from seeing anything at first.

'Anyone at home?' one of the campers called, and the others laughed.

Fanch looked up and started in alarm. In the dim light of a shattered port-hole, a lanky motionless figure lay along one of the starboard bunks. With hands crossed behind the back of his head in the attitude of repose which Fanch recognized, Benny lay watching the boy, his eyes screwed up against the smoke from his cigarette.

'I was expecting you,' he said mockingly. 'We've been on one another's heels for the last ten days, and even if I did beat you here at the finish, I admit I lost overall. It isn't easy to pull the wool over your eyes, and it's really having you on my tail that got me here at all.'

Since they had last met, Pat and Fredo had given him

another beating-up and had managed to black his one sound eye, the left. However, this did at least balance his sallow face.

Fanch made an enormous effort to recover himself.

'It can't be! You must have come here on stilts. Or did you get a helicopter to parachute you on to the Seven Marshes?'

'I did this rather exhausting walk before, when I first visited the neighbourhood,' Benny admitted. 'I even walked past the sluice several times without noticing the boat under all these weeds. I'm afraid that the pair of louts I had on my hands were making such a childish fuss that they didn't know where they were. I had to go out of my way to see them safe. I grant you Pat and Fredo are first-rate burglars, but luckily they're lost without their little comforts, and that gave us a tremendous advantage over them.'

Hearing a strange voice alternate with Fanch's, the others came swarming aboard. Benny raised himself lazily on one elbow and pointed to the empty bunk.

'Come right in and make yourselves at home,' he called cheerfully. 'If the boat doesn't exactly belong to me, it certainly belongs to my employers. It's hard to get anything out of the big insurance companies, but once they've paid out on a policy, you can be sure they'll do everything they possibly can to get their money back some other way ... Stop worrying,' he added, 'I'm not a Benafente, you know. Nor am I the crook you think I am. A good Insurance Inspector has got to associate with villains if he wants to make them cough up their loot. For the last six weeks I've been the accomplice of a pretty pair, who've left my face in this sad state. But I won in the end.'

'And what about them?' Monsieur Cogan asked.

'Oh, they're busy getting their breath back in a black maria taking them to Paris. At their journey's end, there'll

135

be three years inside for the crew of the *Waikiki*! I tipped off the police and they were picked up in a restaurant at Sarzeau where they were trying to get over last night's excitement.'

'All the same,' said Blackbeard, 'you could have been a little more careful about the way in which you made use of people like them.'

'When something big is at stake, somebody's bound to get hurt,' was Benny's cynical rejoinder. 'Anyway our raids on Goulvan didn't kill dear old Mamm. Incidentally, I might say she's far handier with a broom than Fredo with a gun.'

He gingerly rubbed his brows. Monsieur Cogan and Lise managed a laugh between them, and so did the two campers, although they had no idea what it was all about. But Fanch's face remained unsmiling. He still did not trust Benny. All five sat in a row on the port bunk, and the campers each produced a foul-smelling pipe. Monsieur Cogan lit a cigarette.

'And what *was* at stake?' he inquired coldly.

'Don't you know?' Benny was amazed. 'The stealing of the cabin-cruiser is a small matter. At any time of the year you may hear of a yacht that slips her moorings with a few fools on board who don't know how to handle her and manage to wreck her within an hour or two. But the *Berenice* carried something immensely precious and once she disappeared all sorts of people began to stir in the underworld.'

'What?' all five asked impatiently.

'Listen, and I'll tell you. It's an amazing story . . . It all started one day last summer in Iraq. An archaeological expedition was digging at Naifur, when one of the native workmen uncovered a golden head of the demi-god Gilgamesh, the hero of Sumerian legend. He shoved it into his barrow under a load of bricks and tipped it on to the rubbish-heap. He crept back after dark and sold it for a hundred pounds to one of the dealers hanging round the gates of the camp. It's almost a tradition out there for these gentry to come flocking round like carrion crows as soon as a dig gets under way . . . '

'But a hundred pounds!' Monsieur Cogan exclaimed. 'Giving it away!'

'Well, that's the original price fetched by the head of Gilgamesh, a masterpiece of Assyrian art, weighing three hundred and thirty-six ounces of pure gold. Mind you, the price has since spiralled to bewildering heights as the head passed from hand to hand. A broker in Baghdad bought it from the Naifur dealer for five thousand dollars, pushed off to Beirut at once where he had excellent contacts and resold it for *fifty* thousand dollars to a group of intermediaries. The latter discreetly passed the news on to their richest customers and word of the new discovery began to circulate in the secret world of the collectors of antiquities. After a couple of months in Beirut, Gilgamesh moved on to Athens and there was visited for the first time by the experts. He found a taker, too, at two hundred thousand dollars . . . '

Manoel and Picou removed the pipes from their mouths to give an admiring whistle.

'The five buyers raised the money between them,' Benny went on. 'They were links in a chain which led back to Paris, to the gloomy basement of a small antique shop in the Rue Dragon. The place doesn't look up to much, but the owner has his contacts. There the bearded god was examined and authenticated by experts. When that was done, he was dated, photographed from all angles, had a cast taken of himself and was fitted out with an ebony cabinet lined with red velvet . . . '

'So you've seen it?' Lise asked.

'Never set eyes on it,' Benny answered bitterly. 'Except

in photographs. There were some in several art magazines.'

'What happened next?' Fanch asked. 'Was Gilgamesh long in Paris?'

'Barely a month ... His picture was enough to make three wealthy American collectors decide that they simply had to acquire the bearded god. After a transatlantic jet-flight they turned up one after the other in the shop in the Rue Dragon. Then things really began to hum, but the upshot of it all was that a millionaire Philadelphia banker, Lew Gibson, secured the piece for five hundred thousand dollars and at once insured it properly for that amount. The next thing he did was to nip down to Deauville with the head in an endeavour to recover the purchase price at the gaming-tables. That very evening, while Lew was trying in vain to break the bank at the Casino, a couple of jokers who had been keeping an eye on events, broke into the villa in which he was staying and removed the head. They were Pat and Fredo. Naturally neither of them had any thought of getting five hundred thousand dollars out of Gilgamesh. But they knew perfectly well (and this has happened before) that insurance companies will pay a quarter of the value of an insured article and ask no questions if it is returned safely. To secure their escape, and their crossing to England, from where it would be far easier to negotiate, they brought into the plot the paid-hand on a large cabin-cruiser. The owner was away, so it was easy for them to slip her moorings ...'

'Now we're coming to it!' Fanch rubbed his hands. 'This is where Benafente and the *Berenice* come into the picture.'

'Quite right,' Benny went on. 'They left Trouville Harbour in the middle of the night, but their haste was so suspicious that they were hailed from the quay and from vessels tied up alongside. Luckily for them the weather was simply dreadful, something which suited the schemes of the cunning Benafente. It was the easiest thing in the world for him to alter course without the others realizing it. They were novices, visibility was nil, and anyway they were utterly laid out by sea-sickness. In the dim light of dawn, one day towards the end of March, the cruiser slipped like a ghost through the straits of Port-Navalo. Nobody saw her come in, and she wandered round the maze of islands in the gulf on the extra-high equinoctial tide. Thanks to this, Benafente was able to run ashore way up the estuary in the lonely spot where we are now. And his two passengers were so sea-sick that they mistook the way into the Little Sea for the entrance to Plymouth Harbour!'

He paused for a moment to join the others' laughter. Fanch, meanwhile, was beginning to wonder whether Benafente, the piratical sailor, and Benny Cosquer, the private inquiry agent in the insurance company's pay, were not, after all, one and the same person.

Benny went on.

'Pat and Fredo took fright once more, hastily paid off their accomplice and got ashore with their precious box, leaving Benafente to deal with the *Berenice* as best he could. When at last, some two hours later, they emerged from this diabolical maze of mud and water, they got a nasty shock when they found they were not on the Exeter bypass as they had hoped, but on the deserted road to Vannes. They got an even nastier shock that evening back in Paris when they opened the box and found that Gilgamesh had vanished, replaced by a lump of lead Benafente had removed from the ballast in the hold.'

'How do you know all this?' Monsieur Cogan asked suspiciously.

'Benafente told us himself! A few weeks later, when news of the robbery was still hitting the headlines, he very discreetly contacted our offices and opened negotiations.

"The bearded god is on the bottom of the River Noyalo. If you want to know exactly where he is, you'd better pay me first." Well, we bought his map from him and paid him a good price for his information and he passed out of the story. The next thing that happened was that Pat and Fredo got in touch with us through a third party. Things were beginning to take shape. We had only the barest chance of recovering Gilgamesh, and our strongest card was its extraordinary value. It's practically impossible to negotiate the sale of a unique work of art at that price, unless your reputation is good.'

'Did those two thugs make as much out of it as Benafente?' Fanch asked.

'Not a penny! The best tactics an insurance company can employ are to place their observers in the right spots, let the crooks do all the hard work of treasure-hunting and then pounce when they've found what they're looking for. So a month later I met those two and pretended I was a pal of Benafente. My story was that he was doing time for another offence and that he had sent me to see his old accomplices and help them recover Gilgamesh, with the proviso that the loot was to be split three ways. It was to our joint advantage to combine, because the information I had complemented their own. We reached an agreement, and turned up here in June to look for the wreck of the *Berenice*. Fanch knows the rest of the story as well as I do.'

'And where is Gilgamesh?' the others asked in unison.

A look of bitter disappointment swept over Benny's battered face.

'I've just turned the whole boat inside out and there's no sign of him . . . If you don't believe me, look yourselves: it won't take you long.'

'Perhaps Benafente got here first,' Blackbeard suggested.

Benny shook his head.

'He's well out of the running ... Got killed in a café brawl in Nice last month. The only thing for us to do now is to dredge the whole marsh very carefully, or at least down to where Fanch found the dinghy from the yacht. And that'll take us several weeks.'

Monsieur Cogan still looked unconvinced.

'What proof have you that Benafente didn't take the head of Gilgamesh away from here? After all, he'd have picked up a lot more if he'd walked into your offices and deposited the statue on your chairman's desk.'

'And run a far bigger risk!' Benny replied. 'No, but it may well be that, in his written statement, Benafente only told us part of the truth. He claimed that after he had put a lump of lead in the box in place of the head, he hid the real head behind the engines. I've looked everywhere and Gilgamesh just isn't here. I can only suppose that the sailor wanted to make sure of an extra reward by delaying the discovery of the head. Before he made off he must have found another hiding-place for Gilgamesh, either round here or on the nearer bank, but I very much fear we'll never find it.'

Suddenly he looked hard at Fanch. The latter seemed lost in thought.

'You really were a silly little fool to scuttle that dinghy. Benafente must have used it to get ashore and he may have scratched something interesting on the hull, something to jog his memory about where he had finally hidden the god.'

'You'd believe in Father Christmas if you think that,' Fanch retorted. 'We were out one whole morning together and you had plenty of time to examine her from stem to stern. What do you think *I*'d find if you noticed nothing? If you ask me, the best thing you can do is to order your dredgers, and get a move on. If the head of Gilgamesh weighs what you said it does, every tide'll sink it another three feet deeper in the mud. After a year it will have rejoined the flints and the potsherds, six times older than the head, that cover the old valley bottom. Put your back into it and you'll soon have those five hundred thousand dollars you had to fork out to the American.'

His scorn made the others laugh, particularly the two campers who were already very disgusted at leaving empty-handed and who dearly wanted to see the head of Gilgamesh so that they could compare his beard with their own.

Benny pointed an accusing finger at Fanch.

'You know something!' he stormed. 'You came up here before anyone else on the Spring tides!'

'Yes, but I never got as far as this,' Fanch said softly. 'And I found myself in real trouble with Monsieur Cogan because of it . . . You misunderstand me completely. I'm not interested in your solid-gold god; I'm just out for fun. Gilgamesh has had a long journey and of course we're all very sorry he's been lost. But if he comes out of the mud one of these days, I hope the first face he sees will be a bit more cheerful than yours.'

8

The Golden Eyes of Gilgamesh

THEREAFTER, life on Goulvan resumed a more peaceful round. Fanch, however, knew that he was being watched. Grey launches with black numbers on their bows sometimes cruised off Sow Bay and sometimes, too, he would see the rubber raft with its powerful outboard engine which was used as a safety boat for the yacht clubs during the summer.

Towards noon one day, Benny Cosquer came over with the two starchy gentlemen whom Fanch had seen that evening on the quay at Locmariaquer. They found Mamm Guidic guarding the gateway, broom in hand.

'Here you are again. What do you want this time?' she asked, somewhat disagreeably.

'We only wanted to pay our respects and have a word or two with Fanch,' Benny answered with suspicious friendliness.

Since they'd last seen him his nose had recovered its old dimensions and his three missing front teeth had miraculously sprouted once more.

'You've timed it well,' Mamm said. 'As it happens, Fanch has something for you.'

Serious and unsmiling, the boy came quietly into the yard carrying a large, and apparently heavy, parcel wrapped in brown paper. The intruders caught their breath and stared.

'No,' Fanch said coldly, 'it isn't the head of Gilgamesh. I'm afraid it's rather late in the day, Monsieur Cosquer, but these are the clothes you asked me to buy for you, at the time of your short stay on Cow Island. Good cheap stuff! Still, they may come in handy when you're dredging the Seven Marshes.'

Benny looked angry as he took the parcel. What disappointed him so much was to find that Fanch had become hostile towards him again. The secret bond formed between them on the morning of their sailing trip had lasted for only a short while. He tried to appeal to the boy again.

'The adventure I told you about the other day isn't over yet. You can still find quite a bit of excitement if you come up to the wreck of the *Berenice* now and again. Both banks are guarded now, but I'll see that no one disturbs you. Wouldn't you like to look for Gilgamesh?'

'I've had enough of that,' Fanch answered carelessly, 'and if I want any excitement, I can get it any day I like racing down the little channel by Ar-Gazek at twelve knots on the ebb tide.'

Benny gave up, puzzled by his ungraciousness.

'I'll be staying a little longer at Locmariaquer,' were his parting words. 'If you do come across anything you think might interest us, let me know via Monsieur Tanguy.'

That was the last they saw of him on Goulvan, and of the glum couple of detectives with him. On the other hand, pleasure and duty had made Blackbeard a permanent fixture in the guest-room.

After Pat and Fredo's last incursion, there was, at certain times of the day, an uneasy feeling about the Guidics' isolation. At the smallest sound of an engine, or even when a sailing-boat came too close to Sow Rock, Uncle Job, or Monsieur Cogan, or Fanch, or even all three together would sneak down to the cove to keep a look-out.

The only visitors admitted to the farm were Manoel and Picou. Mamm Guidic let their Assyrian beards and the cheerful grins behind them seduce her, and with her blessing they were allowed to camp on the eastern end of the island and take more than the occasional meal in the big kitchen with their hosts.

'The story's got out at last,' they told Fanch. 'Yesterday afternoon, as we were coming back from Poteau Rouge, we went out of our way round the Seven Marshes. The place is alive with treasure-hunters in dungarees and frogmen's outfits. Some of them are up to their waists in mud dragging with grapnels.'

From now on the *Petit-Emile* and the yellow canoe set out sailing or fishing together. Long trips took the gang to the green shores of Larmor-Baden or the Vincin estuary, from which they all returned dog-tired but drunk with the sun and the sea air.

But this was only a way of cheating the secret disappointment which they all felt. No one now dared mention the mysterious estuary away over to the east from Goulvan, and Fanch was careful to keep well clear of its neighbourhood.

One morning Mamm Guidic's fifteen Friesians were returning at low tide from Cow Island. They were driven by the dog Merlin and by two cow-boys in shorts who shouted at the tops of their voices as they came splashing through the water. Blackbeard himself led the way, never faltering from the path strewn with glittering pools of water, which for a space linked the islanders to the distant mainland.

The Friesians mooed when they were back in their old pasture between the farm garden, the heath and the barren crown of the cliff-tops. Monsieur Cogan and the boy were just going back to the house when the sound of an engine drew them to the southern tip of the island. The shoals between Goulvan and the Ile-Hervé were completely exposed. Monsieur Jégo was standing up in his big punt, grounded on the edge of the channel, waving his arms in excitement.

'I've got something to show you that'll cheer you up,' he called to Fanch. 'Hurry up and come aboard, there's only half an hour of low water left.'

Lise, who had got up early, stood smiling at his side. Fanch and Blackbeard jumped aboard, Monsieur Jégo put the engine in gear and moved out into the middle of the channel. They went off at top speed until they reached the pickets marking the first oyster-parks.

There they found the wreck of the *Petit-Emile II,* the water slopping over the gunwales, scarcely a hundred yards from the spot where Fanch had scuttled her. Sand and sea had rubbed away part of the pitch which the boy had daubed on her hull and patches of the original white paint showed through.

'At first I thought it was one of Mamm Guidic's cows that had fallen into the water and drowned,' Monsieur Jégo said. 'Here, if you close one eye, doesn't it look just like the corpse of a Friesian?'

Apart from the change of colour, the dinghy seemed little the worse for her submersion. Nobody spoke as they waited to see what Fanch would do. Without hesitation he jumped into the water, and Blackbeard and Lise came after him.

'Chuck me your bailer,' the schoolmaster called to Monsieur Jégo. 'It would be a shame to leave her to rot.'

Ten minutes and the dinghy from the *Berenice* was afloat once more, gently nudging the side of the punt.

Hearing the noise of an engine coming from Sow Bay, Mamm Guidic left the chicken-run and walked to the yard-gate to see what was happening. Her mind was soon at rest; there was Fanch coming up the drive with his friends. They all looked cheerful, though nobody said a word. That sly wretch Fanch always assumed an expression that was too good to be true on the very few occasions when he had some crime to confess or, much more frequently, when he had a favour to beg. The old lady stood firm and tried to keep the twinkle out of her grey eyes.

'Look,' said Fanch most meekly, 'the *Petit-Emile II* has just popped up again at low water off the Jégos' place. In the last hour, masses of people must have passed her, yet nobody's wanted her. And I didn't do anything to make her bob up there. It was all the fault of the tides.'

He looked up and gazed at Mamm with such a satisfied expression on his face that the others could not help laughing.

'Couldn't I keep her just for a few days until Monsieur Cogan goes? With him and Lise aboard it makes the old *Petit-Emile* pretty cramped and our fishing's beginning to suffer. When Monsieur Cogan goes back to Saint-Arzhel, and of course we all hope that won't be for a long time yet, then I'll take the dinghy back to Locmariaquer like the old windbag told me to, and we'll hear no more of it.'

'All right,' said Mamm Guidic. 'But take good care that it doesn't bring the police and the burglars and all that crowd of nasty people who don't belong here. Otherwise I'll get cross.'

The two boats were grounded side by side on the beach while the gear was taken out of one and put into the other. Blackbeard took the opportunity to examine the new boat from stem to stern, since it was the first time he had seen her. There was nothing mysterious about her clean lines and nothing to show that she had played any part whatsoever in the disappearance of Gilgamesh. When the old dinghy had been cleared, the new one was hauled into the water to become the *Petit-Emile* once more as she floated free. The tide was slowly filling Sow Bay. The sides of the cove were fresh and green in the morning sun. A land breeze had sprung up and as this harbinger of fine weather blew from the Séné peninsula it ruffled the sea a darker blue.

The change-over tempted Blackbeard to put to sea at once with Fanch. They spent some time tacking between the rocks and the pine-crowned point.

Lise had stayed aboard the now-despised old dinghy, sitting in the bows, disentangling the hand-lines, still wet from their last fishing trip, coiling them on their frames and tucking in the hooks. Soon the tide began to lift the *Petit-Emile* and she began to float beside her mooring buoy, dragging at the anchor chains and bumping into the old oil-drum with a resounding *boom*. The dinghy behaved like a horse eager to leave its stable.

Lise finished her task, lulled by the lazy movement, and then leaned over the bows to watch the tide coming in. Each wave reshaped the pattern of the sand, stirring it up into a mist as it rubbed out the lines left by the ebb and brought back the familiar seaweed, crabs, empty shells and small fish of the water's edge.

Her face framed by her fair hair stared back at her like a mermaid under the prow. Then, as she leaned still farther over to smile at her own reflection, the sand-clouded water cleared for a moment and another shadowy face looked up through her own. As each wave passed, a pair of golden eyes stared up at her from the bottom a few feet down.

Blackbeard was at the tiller of the other boat. He put about as soon as Lise's cry came shrilling across the water. She remained in the same position, leaning right over the bows, hypnotized by the fleeting glimmer that came and went with the ebb and flow of the waves. At last the shadow of the red sail blotted out this strange mirage.

'You gave us a fright,' Fanch said. 'What's the matter?'

Lise didn't look up.

'Gilgamesh,' she said in a choked voice. 'He's here, right under the bows.'

Monsieur Cogan and the boy both leaned impetuously over the side.

'I can only see the bottom,' said Blackbeard.

'She's just imagining things,' Fanch muttered. 'There's nothing there, only the anchor weights for the mooring-buoy.'

Then his jaw sagged as though the breath had suddenly been knocked out of his body. Monsieur Cogan turned and noticed his odd expression.

'Fanch, you look as though you'd suddenly remembered something . . . What's up?'

'Benny was wrong, the other evening, when he said that what Pat and Fredo found in the ebony casket was a lump of ballast. Those two idiots didn't look closely enough before they got rid of it . . . You remember when we went over the *Berenice*? I was the only one who went over her really thoroughly with a seaman's eye . . .'

'Granted,' Blackbeard admitted. 'So what?'

'Well, what struck me was that to get at the ballast you've got to do what I did – pull up one of the floor-boards. As the cabin runs the full length of the boat, you couldn't do that without being seen by the passengers. So I'm sure Benafente must have used something else to weight the coffer.'

'But what?'

'I don't quite know, but it could have been the mooring-block from the dinghy.'

Monsieur Cogan's eyes widened.

'It would have been a chunk of stone or concrete,' Fanch went on, 'and as he couldn't get at the ballast on the *Berenice* he must have used the mooring-block from the dinghy, that is if it was the right shape and weight to go in the coffer.'

'All right,' said Blackbeard, 'but we're no further forward by knowing that Pat and Fredo carefully carried off a lump of concrete instead of the head of a god worth five hundred thousand dollars . . . What are you getting at?'

He was annoyed by Fanch's roundabout reasoning. Lise, meanwhile, was still leaning over the water vainly looking for the golden eyes which had disappeared under the shadow of the sail. Fanch went on.

'There was a concrete mooring-block in the bottom of the dinghy when I hauled her out of the mud,' he muttered. 'It was a black-painted cylinder of a thing with a steel ring coming out of it on the end of a wire rope.'

He held his hands apart to show its dimensions and Blackbeard at once guessed what was in his mind.

'What did you do with it?'

'Well, as the mooring block really belonged with the dinghy, I took it back to Goulvan and never gave it another thought. It was a good weight, and I used it to double the anchor block of our mooring-buoy. It often used to get shifted by the ebb . . . Here, quick, give me a hand.'

They hurried forward and spun the old black oil-drum round. Fanch grabbed the chain and hauled it in hand over hand until he reached the crowsfoot. Then each took a separate cable and began hauling in. All Blackbeard brought up, however, was a rusty anchor and he threw it over the side again in disgust.

'It's this one,' Fanch said, red in the face from his exertions. 'Come and give me a hand.'

Some malignant spirit seemed to be keeping the mooring-block on the bottom and they both had to heave with all their strength. But at last it came away and rose spinning through the cloudy water. Lise gave another shout. Up came Gilgamesh, the water streaming off him as he

half emerged from the blackish matrix which the slow steady action of the waves had partially worn away.

Scared by their catch, the two anglers abruptly jerked it aboard as if it had been some big fish. As it fell on the floorboards, the concrete which enveloped the bearded god dropped away and he lay completely exposed, grinning in the sunlight. Lise stepped from one boat to the other so as to see him better. The glory of their prize silenced the three of them. At first they looked at him from a respectful distance, not daring to touch the golden face which stared at them so serenely.

'Half a million dollars!' Monsieur Cogan sighed. 'Why not half a million brass farthings? To those who value the past, you can't put a price on a marvellous thing like this.'

Lise had lived through the most exciting moments of their discovery.

'You haven't seen anything really,' she told the others. 'He was so much more beautiful and so much more terrible under the water. I'm half disappointed now you've fished him up.'

Happy and relieved by the way in which things had turned out, Fanch's only thought was to make a harmless little joke.

'We could give him to Mamm,' he said with a chuckle. 'Only we couldn't call him Gilgamesh. If we said he was Saint Gildas, she'd set him on the mantelpiece straight away.'

It dripped salt water all the way back to the farm, and when Mamm Guidic saw Blackbeard nursing the golden statue in his arms as though it were a baby, she shouted at him in rage.

'I'm not having that thing in my house! Take the horrible object away and drop it over the side on the deepest part of the channel.'

'That would be a shame,' Monsieur Cogan pleaded.

'Well then, get it on the boat and take it over to Loc-mariaquer at once. You can leave the golden head and the white dinghy with people who are used to dealing with that sort of thing ... I'm not having the newspapers taking the name of the Ile-Goulvan in vain!'

Monsieur Tanguy lowered the binoculars for a moment to rest his weary eyes, then once more scanned the elegant white sails cutting the sea off Locmariaquer. It was noon, the time of the daily conference in the Harbour Master's tiny office. For the past few days he had left it to the Customs man to keep his visitors at bay. Suddenly a red sail, squarer than the others, drew his attention.

'Would you believe it?' he said bitterly. 'There he is again, that wrecker from Goulvan, and he is this very instant venturing into our waters. The notice on the wharf ought to make him mind his manners.'

Benny Cosquer, the police, the Coastguards and Monsieur Stephani crowded eagerly to the window.

'That Fanch is a bird of ill omen,' Old Hogshead told them as he watched through his glasses. 'You can bet he's only come across to get what he can out of some fresh disaster ... It's a pity times have changed. A few hundred years ago I could have met that pirate with a volley of grapeshot. All I can do now is put on my cap and show him politely up to my office.'

He came downstairs and through the Café Poder, knocking back a glass of Muscadet en route to sharpen his wits, and walked over to the quayside, cursing the lawless islanders who made fun of all the local by-laws.

Fanch was hardly surprised to see his brick-red face peering down over the harbour wall. He was sportsman enough to appreciate the old sailor's eyes which were as keen as ever.

'Am I dreaming?' Monsieur Tanguy called down

indignantly to him. 'Or has the *Petit-Emile* come to life for a second time . . . This really is something! All you have to do is stamp your foot and your boat doubles her tonnage straight away. Come up to the office with me, my lad, and I'll lay such a string of charges against you you'll never play another practical joke for the rest of your life.'

Fanch appeared empty-handed in front of his gloomy judges gathered on the first floor. After him came Blackbeard, carrying Gilgamesh wrapped in a tattered blanket. Lise sheltered timidly behind them. She did not wish to miss the last act of the crazy farce played round the stolen treasure.

'What have you brought me now?' Benny asked wearily. 'I suppose I left something in that shed on Cow Island . . .'

None of the three uttered a word. Monsieur Cogan laid his burden on the desk and removed its covering. The sight of the grinning bearded god hit the gentlemen like a bolt from the blue. One of them, keeping a cooler head than the others, pounded downstairs to telephone Lorient and countermand the orders to the suction-dredgers. The others meanwhile stammered meaningless strings of words as they handled the treasure. It passed back and forth from hand to hand like a rugby ball down a three-quarter line.

'Where did you find it?' someone asked.

Fanch craftily left it to Blackbeard to describe their discovery in detail. For a moment Benny's beaky nose swung threateningly in the boy's direction. Then the certainty of success drove away the suspicions that still lingered behind his expressionless face.

'What about the dinghy?' Fanch asked as they were leaving. He wanted everything to be official. 'What shall I do with her?'

'I should keep her, if I were you,' Benny answered abstractedly. 'You can willingly have her.'

'Done!' said Fanch quickly. 'But sign a proper paper for me right away. I don't want any more trouble from Old . . .'

'Old who?' Old Hogshead asked, his purple nose quivering.

Fanch swiftly moved over to the desk where Benny drew up and signed the transfer document, a large rubber stamp making it legal.

'Happy now?' he asked, pushing the paper across the desk to the boy. 'You've got what you wanted.'

Fanch nodded.

'And so have you. But I'm sure you won't be entirely happy to leave the Little Sea . . . why not go sick this winter and come down to convalesce on Goulvan? You'll enjoy yourself and Mamm still has a soft spot for you.'

'I certainly won't say no,' Benny answered thoughtfully.

Not knowing quite how to say good-bye to the others, Fanch backed away with Blackbeard and Lise each tugging at an elbow. Then they were off without so much as a backward glance at the golden eyes of Gilgamesh.

Below, the *Petit-Emile* bumped impatiently at the quayside. Lise was on the verge of tears and Blackbeard felt sorry for her.

'You mustn't be upset, my dear,' he said softly. 'Your cry awoke Gilgamesh this morning on the beach at Goulvan.'

'Oh . . . oh . . .' Lise sobbed, 'I did want to keep him a little longer.'

'You'll see him again, I expect, in a museum,' Fanch said as he cast off.

He was bubbling with mirth, like a boy who has managed to pull off the biggest joke in his life. Suddenly Blackbeard understood what was behind this excessive exuberance.

'I suppose you think it's funny to have had the cops *and* robbers running round in circles?' he said. 'You've known all along what was anchoring the buoy twelve feet away from that rusty old anchor in Sow Bay.'

'So what?' Fanch burst out laughing. 'It didn't kill anyone to wait a little. Why, we could have kept those boys on the hop all summer.'

Lise was left to watch the helm while they argued furiously.

'Do you want us to go back and see the captain right away?' Blackbeard was saying threateningly.

'That wouldn't help anyone. It's finished and done with now; the treasure-hunters are all satisfied: Lew Gibson will get his old god back once he forks out five hundred thousand dollars to the insurance company, plus expenses: Benny'll get a fat reward: those other miserable so-and-so's will all get promoted for doing nothing, and Old Hogshead'll have his picture in all the papers.'

Monsieur Cogan gave way.

'All right, let's forget about it . . . But, tell me truthfully, when did you find Gilgamesh?'

Fanch turned and stared at him.

'One evening last month,' he said. 'I was mooring the *Petit-Emile* to the buoy. There wasn't a breath of wind and the water was as clear as glass. At first when I saw his golden eyes blinking up at me from the bottom, I never connected him with the mooring-block I'd salvaged from the dinghy. It was only when I hauled in the cables as we did just now, that I realized what had come my way.'

'Well, well!' Blackbeard growled. 'Why didn't you tell someone?'

'I'd no idea what was going on: I was completely in the dark about it then. I had to wait and see who and what would turn up. And I didn't have to wait long! Meanwhile, all I could do was bury the wretched thing as deep as I could in the sand. Every time the tide ebbed, Uncle's big punt dragged her moorings, and out of the sand popped a bit of the god's beard. So I had to do the job all over again twice a day. I wasn't having any old beachcomber grabbing the prize from under my nose.'

Monsieur Cogan wanted to laugh, but he managed to keep a straight face.

'You've behaved very badly!'

'Mamm won't be cross with me,' Fanch retorted calmly. 'It's not a secret, I've only been keeping a promise.'

'And what was it?' Blackbeard asked more gently.

Fanch reddened.

'Ever since we were children,' he said, 'Lise's always asked me to find her a treasure. I only kept quiet about this one, to give her the joy of finding it herself.'

In his confusion Blackbeard turned towards Lise. Her hair blew about her face; she gave an odd little smile.

'Don't let them fool you,' she said simply. 'Fanch was the one who was right . . .'

And she pointed towards the boundless horizon of the Little Sea, the glitter of the tide-bound islands and the *Petit-Emile*'s red sail swelling triumphantly above their heads.

About the Author

Paul Berna was born at Hyères in 1913. He was the youngest son of a large, noisy, and quarrelsome family where everybody had a good deal of fun. He spent the whole of his childhood in the South of France, and though circumstances have forced him to spend a lot of time elsewhere he has always been very attached to this part of the country.

He went to school in Toulon and later at Aix, where he did very well, passing his pre-university exam with credit. His great interest in books and literature of every kind went hand in hand with an enthusiasm for football and swimming. After leaving school he did a two year apprenticeship at a Paris bank. This was followed by a number of jobs, none of which really appealed to him. After the Second World War he was offered an administrative job in the Post Office.

In spite of his professional occupations he has always been interested in young people and their books. Indeed, all his works show that he has a remarkable insight into the mind of the modern child.

In 1960 he married Saint-Marcoux who is well known for her novels for older girls.

A Hundred Million Francs, The Street Musician, The Knights of King Midas, The Mystery of the Cross-eyed Man, and *Flood Warning* are all available in Puffins.

If you have enjoyed this book and would like to know about others which we publish, why not join the Puffin Club? You will be sent the Club magazine *Puffin Post* four times a year and a smart badge and membership book. You will also be able to enter all the competitions. Write for an application form to:

The Puffin Club Secretary
Penguin Books Limited
Bath Road
Harmondsworth
Middlesex